Arthur Wing Pinero

Sweet Lavender

A Comedy in Three Acts

Arthur Wing Pinero

Sweet Lavender
A Comedy in Three Acts

ISBN/EAN: 9783744787482

Printed in Europe, USA, Canada, Australia, Japan

Cover: Foto ©Andreas Hilbeck / pixelio.de

More available books at **www.hansebooks.com**

THE
PLAYS of
ARTHUR W. PINERO

EET LAVENDER

COMEDY IN THREE ACTS.

Acting Rights Reserved.

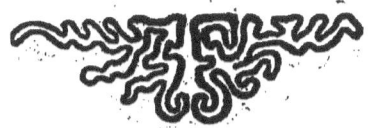

'ALTER H. BAKER & CO.,
BOSTON.

SWEET LAVENDER

A COMEDY IN THREE ACTS

BY

ARTHUR W. PINERO

BOSTON

THE PERSONS OF THE PLAY.

HORACE BREAM (*a young American*).

GEOFFREY WEDDERBURN (*of Wedderburn, Green & Hoskett, Bankers, Barnchester*).

CLEMENT HALE (*his adopted son, studying for the Bar*).

RICHARD PHENYL (*a Barrister*).

DR. DELANEY (*a fashionable Physician*).

MR. BULGER (*Hairdresser and Wigmaker*).

MR. MAW (*a Solicitor*).

MINNIE GILFILLIAN (*Niece of Mr. Wedderburn*).

RUTH ROLT (*Housekeeper and Laundress at No. 3, Brain Court, Temple*).

LAVENDER (*her daughter*).

MRS. GILFILLIAN (*a widow — Wedderburn's sister — Minnie's mother*).

THE FIRST ACT.
MORNING. ".NOBODY'S BUSINESS."

THE SECOND ACT.
EVENING OF THE NEXT DAY. "SOMEBODY'S BUSINESS."

THE THIRD ACT.
A WEEK LATER. "EVERYBODY'S BUSINESS."

SCENE.

Chambers of Mr. Phenyl and Mr. Hale, No. 3, Brain Court, Temple, London. Springtime. The Present Day.

AUTHOR'S NOTE.

The author of "Sweet Lavender" begs to remind his American patrons — amongst whom there may be those who are unfamiliar with the mode of life he attempts to depict in this play — that a set of chambers in the precincts of the Temple, though constituting only a portion of a house, is a distinct and separate establishment. Each set of chambers has an independent door opening upon a common stairway, behind which door the occupant of the chambers is as much the lord of a castle as if he were in enjoyment of a mansion or a villa surrounded by a brick wall.

"Chambers" consist of three or four rooms, and perhaps a pantry, and are often shared by two boon companions. The female domestic attached to the house — who flits, not unlike the busy bee, from floor to floor — is, in the phraseology of Temple life, called the "Laundress;" and if, like Ruth Rolt, she dwells upon the premises, she enjoys the further distinction of being the "Housekeeper."

The man who shelters in the Temple precincts obtains a silent security from the conventionalities of society. He is untrammelled, uncriticised, unobserved ; and while he pursues the career, either of a devoted student or an ardent Bohemian, the oaken door which closes upon his rooms shuts him off from the world as conclusively as if he were a monk in a cell.

4

INTRODUCTORY NOTE

" SWEET LAVENDER " must be regarded as one of the most successful stage-plays of modern times, and there can be no question that it has proved so far the most popular of Mr. Pinero's works. Its representations may be counted by the thousand, and its popularity has extended over many latitudes. The reason of this is not far to seek ; it proclaims itself in the gentle humanity and genial humour of the play, and the lovable creation of the golden-hearted, weak-natured, down-at-heel Dick Phenyl. The very simplicity and unpretentiousness of this domestic comedy have apparently disarmed any antagonistic criticism which might have been expected from those critics of cynical temper and pessimistic mood who are wont to look for the stern realities of life even in the most purposely genial of theatrical entertainments. And if these, in view of the preponderance of kindly human nature in the play, elect to regard " Sweet Lavender " as a sort of modern fairy-tale rather than an actual and realistic study of life, certainly no one would be more ready to agree with them than Mr. Pinero himself. He avowedly designed the piece as a pleasant entertainment, and the proof that he accomplished his purpose is the fact of the phenomenally successful career of the work all over the world. Had Mr. Pinero in the early months of 1888 written a play of the order of " The Second Mrs. Tanqueray " for Terry's

5

Theatre, the result would in all probability have been disaster.

" Sweet Lavender " was first produced on Wednesday evening, March 21st, 1888, and was from the first received with so much enthusiasm that at once the playgoing public began to flock to Terry's Theatre. Mr. Pinero's comedy, in fact, drew the town, Mr. Edward Terry's Dick Phenyl became almost a household word, and the play held its place in the programme continuously until January 25th, 1890, by which date it had been performed as many as 683 times. But this was not the end of its career at Terry's Theatre, for, after Mr. Edward Terry's holiday trip to India, the actor-manager signalised his return by a revival of " Sweet Lavender " on October 4th, 1890, and between that date and November 26th of the same year, 54 performances were given, bringing the number of representations at this house up to 737.

The following copy of the first night's programme of the original production at Terry's will be interesting for future reference: _____

TERRY'S THEATRE,

105 & 106 STRAND.

Sole Lessee and Manager, Mr. Edward Terry.

_____

WEDNESDAY, MARCH 21, 1888,

FOR THE FIRST TIME,

An Original Domestic Drama, in Three Acts, entitled

SWEET LAVENDER,

BY

A. W. PINERO.

6

MR. GEOFFREY WEDDERBURN (of
Wedderburn, Green & Hoskett,
Bankers, Barnchester) . . . Mr. BRANDON THOMAS.
CLEMENT HALE (his adopted Son,
studying for the Bar) . . . Mr. BERNARD GOULD.
Dr. DELANEY (a fashionable Phy-
sician) . . . . . Mr. ALFRED BISHOP.
DICK PHENYL (a Barrister) . . Mr. EDWARD TERRY.
HORACE BREAM (a young American) Mr. F. KERR.
MR. MAW (a Solicitor) . . . Mr. SANT MATTHEWS.
MR. BULGER (Hairdresser and Wig-
maker) . . . . . Mr. T. C. VALENTINE.
MRS. GILFILLIAN (a Widow — Mr.
Wedderburn's Sister) . . Miss M. A. VICTOR.
MINNIE (her Daughter) . . . Miss MAUDE MILLETT.
RUTH ROLT (Housekeeper and
Laundress at 3 Brain Court,
Temple) . . . . . Miss CARLOTTA ADDISON
LAVENDER (her daughter) . . Miss NORREYS.

ACT I.

NOBODY'S BUSINESS.

Morning.

INTERVAL OF TEN MINUTES.

ACT II.

SOMEBODY'S BUSINESS.

Evening of the next day.

INTERVAL OF TWELVE MINUTES.

7

ACT III.

EVERYBODY'S BUSINESS.

A week afterwards.

---

*Scene: Chambers of Mr. Phenyl and Mr. Hale, 3 Brain Court,
Temple.*

SPRINGTIME—THE PRESENT DAY.

SCENE DESIGNED AND PAINTED BY T. W. HALL.

Mr. T. W. Robertson, who, as a manager and actor of
considerable provincial experience, was prompt to recognise the certain popularity of " Sweet Lavender " with the
immense playgoing public outside the metropolis, at Christ-
mas 1888 commenced a series of provincial tours with
Mr. Pinero's play, and these tours lasted until November
5th, 1891, 697 performances having been given in the
meanwhile. Since then other travelling companies have
performed the play many hundred times all over the
United Kingdom, and it finds a continuously appreciative
public.

In America Mr. Pinero's famous comedy has become a
stock piece, and its representations have been countless
since Mr. Daniel Frohman first produced it at the Lyceum
Theatre, New York. Australia has also taken very
kindly to the play, which was first introduced to Antipo-
dean audiences by Mr. Frank Thornton, and, during
Mr. Edward Terry's recent visit to the colony, " Sweet
Lavender " was naturally expected from him as its original

8

producer, and it was received with enthusiasm at his hands. In South Africa it has also enjoyed frequent representation; in the West Indies it has been much in favour; and Mr. Thornton will shortly take the play to India.

But " Sweet Lavender," like " The Profligate " and " The Magistrate," has appealed beyond the English-speaking body of playgoers to those of the Teutonic and Italian tongues. It has been very frequently performed in Germany in an adaptation which eliminates the sentimental interest to a large extent and lays greater stress on the comic; while the Italian stage knows it also by a version from the pen of a well-known Italian writer. Furthermore, " Sweet Lavender " was recently acted in Russia by a company organised for the purpose of presenting English plays in that country.

MALCOLM C. SALAMAN.

October, 1893.

9

BETWEEN 23D AND 24TH STREETS.

DANIEL FROHMAN........................Manager.

PINERO'S COMEDY.

SWEET LAVENDER.

Horace Bream ....Herbert Kelcey
Geoffrey Wedderburn......................Charles Walcot
Clement Hale...............................Henry Miller
Dick Phenyl................................W. J. LeMoyne
Dr. Delaney............................T. C. Valentine
Mr. Bulger................................W. B. Royston
Mr. Maw................................Walter Bellows
Minnie Gilfillian............... ......Miss Georgia Cayvan
Ruth Rolt...................... ....Mrs. Charles Walcot
Lavender..................... ....Miss Louise Dillon
Mrs. Gilfillian.... ....Mrs. Thomas Sniffen

ACT I.—Morning—Nobody's business.
ACT II.—The next day, evening; somebody's business.
ACT III.—A week afterward—Everybody's business.
PLACE—Chambers of Mr. Phenyl and Mr. Hale, No. 3 Brian Court, temple. TIME.—Springtime, the present day

Boxes.............$10 $12. | Dress Circle and Balcony
Orchestra................$1.50 | (up stairs) $1.50, 1 00, .75 .50
General Admission......... ....$1.00

SUNDAY, JANUARY 8, 1905.

MR. TERRY AS DICK PHENYL.

"Sweet Lavender."

The delicious comedy of "Sweet Lavender," written by Mr. Pinero and representative of his earlier and better style, has been known on our stage for more than sixteen years, and known only to be admired. Last night it was acted at the Princess Theatre, Edward Terry impersonating Dick Phenyl, of which part he was the original representative, and, in view of the superlative power and beauty of this comedian's performance,—a fabric of facile art, combining character, humor, and pathos, at their flood tide of affluence and meaning,—it may be thought that, to the American public, the play now stands for the first time fully revealed. It was received, with every mark of favor, by a crowded house, and the delighted assemblage was kept in almost continual laughter and more than once suddenly moved to tears. Those observers who would comprehend all that is meant by the name of Phenyl should glance for a moment at Longfellow's noble poem of "The Goblet of Life." Phenyl is indeed the image of an experience that is most bitter, and yet, in its result, most beautiful. Edward Terry, a consummate artist, never either excessive or deficient, and adroit to produce the amplest effects by a method of absolute simplicity, impersonates this character with all his heart, as well as all his mind. It seemed easy. Perfect art always does. It is only when you look back upon such acting and thoughtfully consider the fabric of it that you appreciate the difficulty of creating and sustaining such a complex personality and diffusing such a potent charm of lovely illusion. The impersonation of Phenyl by Edward Terry is distinctly and eminently a work of genius. The ideal is clear; the expression of it vigorous with the strength of innate goodness; the humor spontaneous; the feeling deep; the form a symmetrical compound of characteristic traits. No one who knows anything about the art of acting can see this performance without profound admiration of the actor and—which is far more important—without being made happier and better. Mr. Terry's success with the audience was beyond question and conclusive. His high rank as a comedian needs no other vindication. He made a graceful speech, at the close, after several recalls, spoke of "Sweet Lavender" as indeed "a dear, sweet, good old play," and expressed the hope that

SWEET LAVENDER

THE FIRST ACT

The scene is the comfortably furnished sitting-room of some barristers' chambers at 3 Brain Court, Temple. On the spectator's left and right are the doors leading respectively to the bedrooms of RICHARD PHENYL *and* CLEMENT HALE. *At the further end of the room, on the left, is a cur-*
.tained opening leading into a kind of passage, where a butler's tray stands, and facing the outer door of the chambers. The corresponding part of the room, where the windows look on to the Court, forms a kind of recess curtained off from the rest.
It is a bright spring morning.

RUTH ROLT, *a slim, delicate-looking woman of about 35, with a sweet face and a sad soft voice, humbly but very neatly dressed, is laying the breakfast things upon the table.*

BULGER, *a meek bald-headed man, carrying a little old leather bag, a brass pot of hot water, and some clean towels, enters quietly.*

BULGER.
I've give Mr. 'Ale a nice shave, Mrs. Rolt — clean

5

and quick. Water's 'ot enough for me jist to run over Mr. Phenyl's face if 'e's visible.

RUTH.

I'm afraid Mr. Phenyl isn't well enough for you this morning, Mr. Bulger.

BULGER.

Not one of 'is mornin's, hey ?

[RUTH *goes to the right-hand door and knocks sharply.*

RUTH.

[*Calling.*] Mr. Phenyl ! Mr. Phenyl ! The barber.

BULGER.

[*Mildly behind his hand.*] 'Airdresser.

RUTH.

Hairdresser. [*With a mournful shake of the head.*] No use.

BULGER.

Well, Mrs. Rolt, I do wonder at a sooperior young gentleman like Mr. 'Ale stoopin' to reside with one of Mr. Phenyl's sort.

RUTH.

[*Firing up.*] What do you mean ? One of Mr. Phenyl's sort !

BULGER.

I mean a person who's seen staggerin' 'ome with uncertain footfalls at all hours of the mornin', and can't 'old up his 'ead for shavin' more than twice a week.

RUTH.

I shouldn't wonder if Mr. Hale finds something to like, something to respect in Mr. Phenyl, with all his faults.

BULGER.

P'raps so. But to reflect that Mr. 'Ale used to be such a swell, as the sayin' goes, over in Pear Tree Court; and then, three weeks back, to come 'ere and take up with the untidiest chin in the Inner Temple — it's bewilderin'.

RUTH.

[*Impatiently.*] Oh! [*Walks up to the window, where she stands waiting for* BULGER *to go.*]

BULGER.

[*With a sigh.*] Good mornin', Mrs. Rolt.

RUTH.

[*Without turning.*] Good morning.

[BULGER, *on his way to the door, pauses, deposits his brass pot and towels on the table, then opens his bag mournfully.*

RUTH.

[*Turning with surprise.*] Mr. Bulger!

BULGER.

I'm still 'oping, Mrs. Rolt.

RUTH.

It's good to be hoping for something in this world, Mr. Bulger.

BULGER.

[*Taking a piece of paper out of his bag and advancing towards* RUTH.] My affection for you has now took poetic form, ma'am. Will you accept the heartiest effort ?

RUTH.

No, thank you. I —

BULGER.

Think, Mrs. Rolt. When it comes to poetry it comes to something. I, Edmund Bulger, widower, have loved you, Mrs. Ruth Rolt, widow, ever since you fust set foot in the Temple, fifteen years ago, a-bearing your two-year-old baby in your arms, ma'am.

RUTH.

[*Pained.*] Don't — don't.

BULGER.

I was the fust wot ever put scissors to your little Lavender's silky head, Mrs. Rolt.

RUTH.

Yes, I know that.

BULGER.

And I've had the 'andlin' of your tresses too — ay, and the singein' of 'em — till I found I loved you too fond to do your 'air what I call justice. [*Gloomily offering his verses.*] And now it's come down to poetry.

RUTH.

[*Turning away.*] It's no good, indeed.

BULGER.

[*Surveying the paper doubtfully.*] It ain't much good, but intellectually it's my all, ma'am. You won't ?

RUTH.

No, Mr. Bulger, please.

BULGER.

[*Putting away the paper and taking up his things.*] Adjourned *sine die*, ma'am. [*Turning solemnly.*] I take leave for to mention that Mr. Justice Tyler's noo wig which I sent 'ome yesterday nips him at the nap o' the neck. Also that I cut Mr. Pritchett, the emment Q.C.'s chin, in his own chambers yesterday ; a mole as I've skipped over these ten years like a gladsome child. I don't want to make a mountain out of a mole, Mrs. Rolt, but these facts denote the failin' 'and, ma'am. Good mornin'.

[*As* BULGER *is going there is a knock at the outside door, which he opens, and admits* DR. DELANEY, *a genial old Irish gentleman with silvery-grey hair and whiskers.*

DR. DELANEY.

Thank ye — I'm much obliged to ye. I'm calling on Mr. Hale. [BULGER *goes out.*] Is it Mrs. Rolt ?

RUTH.

Yes, sir.

DR. DELANEY.

I'm Doctor Delaney. I've just had the pleasure of seeing your daughter downstairs in the kitchen — in the basement.

RUTH.

My daughter?

DR. DELANEY.

The fact is I'm a friend of Mr. Hale's, and when I met him a night or two back at a little party, he told me that the child of his laundress — of the lady who moinds the house where he has chambers — was looking a little peaky, and that if ever I was near the Temple —

RUTH.

Oh, how good of Mr. Hale!

DR. DELANEY.

Oh, deloightful of him.

RUTH.

[*Gratefully.*]   And you too, Doctor.

DR. DELANEY.

[*Taking her two hands in his for a moment.*] Don't speak of it — not a bit.   Mr. Hale isn't out of his bed yet, I take it?

RUTH.

Yes, Doctor, he'll breakfast in a minute.
[*She goes to a door and knocks.*

DR. DELANEY.

[*To himself.*]   Now I wonder whether this boy is smitten with the bit of a girl downstairs.   Ah! thank goodness, it's no business of mine!

RUTH.

[*Knocking again.*]   Mr. Hale!

CLEMENT.

[*In his room.*] Yes?

RUTH.

Dr. Delaney, please.

CLEMENT.

[*Calling.*] Oh, thank you. I'm coming.
[RUTH *continues laying the table.*

DR. DELANEY.

[*To himself.*] It would be a great disappointment to Wedderburn the banker if the lad he's
adopted did anything absurd. But, thank goodness, it's no business of mine.

RUTH.

Don't you think my girl is looking very pale,
Doctor?

DR. DELANEY.

Ah, don't worry yourself now. It's the air of the
Temple. She's a white chrysanthemum instead
of a pink one. Your daughter's strong enough.

RUTH.

Bless you for telling me that! My Sweet Lavender!

DR. DELANEY.

You're a little pale yourself now.

RUTH.

I — oh, I've had trouble.

DR. DELANEY.

Ah, you're a widow, I'm sorry to hear, Mrs. Rolt.

RUTH.

Yes, Doctor.

DR. DELANEY.

[*To himself.*] And you're right about the trouble you've had if I'm any judge of faces. [*Sadly.*] Thank goodness, it's no business of mine. [*To Ruth.*] Have you been alone a long while ?

RUTH.

[*Coldly.*] I lost Lavender's father before she was born.

DR. DELANEY.

Ah, that's a pity now.

RUTH.

And she's all I have in the world, Doctor. In fact, she's myself. At times I think she's as old as I, or I as young as she. I feel her smile on my face, and the pains and aches I suffer go to her young bones. When she is poring over her lessons at night I am sure my eyes smart, for it —

DR. DELANEY.

Her lessons ! What lessons are those ?

RUTH.

She's a little backward, and works hard with her books in the evening ! Mr. Hale has been good enough to help her.

DR. DELANEY.

Oh, has he ?   And she's very fond of her books —
have ye noticed ?

RUTH.

Yes, very.

DR. DELANEY.

Then the only thing I've got to recommend is
this — that ye'll put a stop to the lessons for six
months or so.

RUTH.

Very well, Doctor.   Poor Lavvy !

DR DELANEY.

[*To himself.*]   I've hit it.   Oh, thank goodness,
this is no business of mine !

CLEMENT HALE *enters.   He is a handsome boyish
young man of about three and twenty. immacu-
lately dressed in a fashionable dressing suit.*

CLEMENT.

Dr. Delaney !

DR. DELANEY.

Mee dear boy !

CLEMENT.

They call you a fashionable physician, and you're
found in the City at ten in the morning.

DR. DELANEY.

Mee dear boy, I'll let you into a secret — we
can't get human ailments to keep fashionable
hours.

CLEMENT.

[*Leading him over to the armchair.*] Best-hearted and best-humoured creature in London, sit in the best chair.

RUTH.

[*To* CLEMENT.] Dr. Delaney has seen Lavender. I — I can't thank you.

CLEMENT.

[*Smiling.*] Please, don't. [*With assumed care-lessness, to* DELANEY.] What do you think of the child?

DR. DELANEY.

[*Hesitatingly.*] Oh — she's been increasing her knowledge a little too rapidly, that's all.

RUTH.

Lavender has to give up her lessons for six months, the Doctor says. Isn't it a pity, Mr. Hale?
[RUTH *goes out.*

CLEMENT.

Give up her lessons?

DR. DELANEY.

Now, it's no good overloading the brain of a young girl. Now, is it?

CLEMENT.

[*Carelessly turning away.*] No, no.

DR. DELANEY.

[*To himself.*] No, nor the heart neither. Good gracious! Here's poor Wedderburn travelling abroad in happy ignorance, and it's nobody's business to look after the boy he loves like a son. Well, it's not *my* business at any rate.

> [*There is the sudden sound of the fall of some heavy object in the adjacent room.*

DR. DELANEY.

What's that now ?

CLEMENT.

That ?   Oh, that's Dick.

DR. DELANEY.

Dick, is it ?

CLEMENT.

Mr. Richard Phenyl, barrister-at-law.   I share his chambers.   Dick's dressing.

DR. DELANEY.

Dropped his waistcoat.

CLEMENT.

Poor Dick !   If you saw him I dare say you'd be shocked at my making a companion of a man like Dick Phenyl.

DR. DELANEY.

Dear me !

CLEMENT.

But I know what good there is in old Dick, and how the good burns clearer and brighter in his slovenly person than in many who've had luck and love and luxury in their lives — which Dick hasn't. I shall pull him round yet.   Like to know him ?

DR. DELANEY.

I loike to know everybody.

CLEMENT.

[*Opening the door slightly.*] Dick! [*To DE-LANEY.*] You won't see him to advantage. I was busy last night, and he ran off the rails a little. Dick! [*Turning away from the door.*] All right.

DICK PHENYL *enters and walks unsteadily towards* CLEMENT. *Dick is a shattered and dissolute-looking man of about five and forty, with shaggy iron-grey hair and ragged whiskers — a pale and cadaverous face, and a suggestion of redness about the nose. He wears the wreck of a once gaudy smoking jacket, which hangs loosely upon him, and his appearance has generally a down-at-heel appearance. But, with all, he presents the remains of a gentleman, and — after he has recovered himself — his manner, though eccentric, is refined and good-humoured.*

DICK.

Clemen', my boy — good mor'ing.

CLEMENT.

[*Reproachfully.*] Hallo, Dick, Hallo!

DICK.

I know wha' you infer, Clemen'. I'm a little late in falling — I mean, in rising, this mor'ing.

CLEMENT.

[*With mock severity.*] A little early in going to bed this morning, Mr. Phenyl.

DICK.

Clemen', my boy, you're so unreasonable. I had an imporrant appointment at the " Steak and Tur-bot," in Flee' Street — a very old-established inn, Clemen' — Doc'or Johnson and all that sor' o' thing. I'm none the worse for it, Clemen'.

CLEMENT.

Are you any the better ?

DICK.

I'm about the same, Clemen'.

CLEMENT.

Let me introduce my friend, Doctor Delaney.

DICK.

Wha' nonsense — Doc'or Johnson.

CLEMENT.

Doctor *Delaney.*

DICK.

[*To* DELANEY.] I beg your par'on — I didn't perceive you when I firs' came in.

> [*He walks rather unsteadily to* DELANEY, *shakes hands with him, then sits on the sofa.*

DR. DELANEY.

Delighted to make your acquaintance, Mr. Phenyl.

DICK.

Than'g you. Were you here when you heard that noise in nex' room ?

DR. DELANEY.

I heard a noise.

DICK.

The pattern on my berrom carpet — dam' 'noying. I had that carpet turned las' week. borrom
upwards — still dam' 'noying pattern. Different
pattern, but pattern. Trip up anybody.

DR. DELANEY.

[*To* CLEMENT.] I happen to have a little something in my pocket that'll pull him together.

CLEMENT.

Give it him, for heaven's sake.

DR. DELANEY.

I want a tumbler.

DICK.

Tum'ler! Tum'ler!

[DICK *goes rapidly to the sideboard and
fetches a tumbler and a decanter of spirits.*

CLEMENT.

[*Quietly.*] Look out.

[DELANEY *takes the tumbler and decanter
from* DICK, *and hands the decanter to*
CLEMENT, *who replaces it on the sideboard. Retaining the tumbler,* DELANEY
*measures into it some drops from a phial
he has taken from his pocket.*

DICK.

[*Mystified.*] Perfec' conjuring trick.

CLEMENT.

[*Offering a carafe of water.*] Water ?

DICK.

[*Quickly.*] Ver' little !

> [DELANEY *pours some water into the tum-*
> *bler, then gives it to* DICK.

DR. DELANEY.

Swallow that, now.

DICK.

Not spirits, I hope — at this hour o' the mor'ing ?

DR. DELANEY.

No, no.

DICK.

[*Annoyed.*] Why not ?

DR. DELANEY.

That's a blessed antidote to the voilest poison
the devil ever put his red seal on — I allude to
Scotch whiskey, not Irish.

DICK.

Wha' nonsense — blessed anecdote.

DR. DELANEY.

Come, come, drink my health, sor.

DICK.

[*Thickly.*] " The Queen ! "

> [DICK *drinks the contents of the tumbler,*
> *then coughs and splutters.*

DR. DELANEY.

How's that, now?

DICK.

Wants keeping another year at least.   Oh!

[DICK *writhes a little as if in pain, then sits on the sofa and buries his head in his hands.*

DR. DELANEY.

He's all right.   I'm off.

RUTH *enters with a tray.*

CLEMENT.

You won't breakfast with us, Dr. Delaney?

DR. DELANEY.

God bless ye for asking me, but I'm very busy over this new hobby of mine.   You've heard of it? "The Home of Forgetfulness!"

CLEMENT.

"The Home of Forgetfulness!"   What's that?

DR. DELANEY.

It's a new home I've endowed for a hundred soft-hearted women who are willing to put themselves at my beck-and-call to nurse the sick and the ailin', rich and poor.   I shall be the commander-in-chief with a trained army at my own barracks.

CLEMENT.

And you do all this alone?

DR. DELANEY.

Ah, why not ? Some of us so-called fashionable physicians have made so much money out of those who haven't anything the matter with 'em that it's hard if we can't do a little for the benefit of those who have.

CLEMENT.

But why "The Home of Forgetfulness"?

DR. DELANEY.

Because it's only by a bed of sickness that many a woman can forget the trouble and pain and disappointment this wurrld has brought her. [*Taking* CLEMENT's *hand.*] God bless ye, mee boy.

CLEMENT.

God bless *you*, Doctor Delaney ! I wish more of us were like you.

DR. DELANEY.

Go along, now. Good-bye. [*Looking at* CLEMENT, *then at* DICK.] Ah, it's no business of mine.

[*He bustles out, brushing past* RUTH.

RUTH.

[*Under her breath to* DELANEY *as he passes her.*] Doctor !

[*He passes through the passage. She following him.*

CLEMENT.

[*Calling after* DELANEY.] Good-bye !

DR. DELANEY.

[*In the distance.*]   Good-bye.

[DICK *having roused himself with a shake and a shiver, looks up, blinking his eyes, his drunkenness gone.*

DICK.

Clem [*going to the table and lifting up the dish-cover*] — Sweetbread — we haven't had breakfast.   [*Calling.*]   Clem !

[CLEMENT *closes the passage door, and drawing the curtain over the opening, comes to the table.*

CLEMENT.

Hallo !

DICK.

[*Severely.*]   You're always late for breakfast, Clement.

CLEMENT.

[*Putting his hand on* DICK'S *shoulder and surveying him.*]   Delaney understands your case, evidently.

DICK.

Delaney ?

CLEMENT.

That was Cormack Delaney, the dear old doctor of Wigmore Street.

DICK.

Oh !   I wish you had introduced me.   Shall we toss for the armchair as usual ?

CLEMENT.

Certainly.

[CLEMENT *tosses a coin and catches it on the back of his hand, covering it.*

CLEMENT.

Call!

[DICK *throws his coin in the air — it falls many yards away from him, but he covers the back of his hand as if he had caught the coin.* CLEMENT *laughs.*

DICK.

[*Uncovering his hand disappointed.*] Oh, never mind — woman!

CLEMENT.

Yours.

[DICK *sits in the armchair.* CLEMENT *helps* DICK *to sweetbread, then pours out tea.*

CLEMENT.

No appetite, I suppose?

DICK.

[*As if with a disagreeable taste in his mouth.*] Hem! I fancy my liver isn't as it should be.

CLEMENT.

Ah! Dick, Dick, you've broken your word to me again.

DICK.

[*Cheerfully.*] The last time, Clement, my boy — the last time.

CLEMENT.

It's always the last time, Dick.

DICK.

[*Making a clatter with his knife and fork, irritably.*] Don't talk childishly. Last night was the last time; it will be the last time. You're invariably finding fault, Clement — it's discouraging. Blame, blame, blame; but praise — oh dear, no!

CLEMENT.

Praise for what?

DICK.

[*Bitterly.*] It is hardly for a man of my age to indicate to a *boy* the particular qualities. [*Appealingly.*] Clem, Clem, I'm sorry — there. I apologise. Never again. [*Holding out his hand.*] Friends, Clement, my boy? Word of honour, my boy.

CLEMENT.

[*Gripping his hand.*] Word of honour, Dick.

DICK.

[*Vigorously.*] Done. But do try to *commend* a little more, Clement — to praise, to encourage. Much may be done by kindness. [*Cheerfully.*] Sweetbread?

CLEMENT.

[*Absently.*] No, thanks, Dick.

DICK.

Off your feed? Spoonful of whiskey in your tea — tone to the stomach.

CLEMENT.

Dick, Delaney says that little Lavender Rolt
ought to discontinue her studies.

DICK.

Oh!

CLEMENT.

[*Leaving the table.*] Confound it! When she is
making such progress.

[CLEMENT *sits with his elbows on the writing-table and his head resting on his hand.*

DICK.

Hallo, Clement, my boy! [*Going over to* CLEM-
ENT *sympathetically.*] This won't do.

CLEMENT.

What won't do?

DICK.

Clem, no man is quite so sober as the individual
who is occasionally otherwise. All his acuteness is
concentrated upon his brief lucid intervals, and in
those intervals his acuteness is — devilish. [*Laying his hand on* CLEMENT'S *shoulder.*] Clement!

CLEMENT.

Dick!

DICK.

When you took compassion upon a worthless,
broken-down reprobate — I allude to the gentleman
now honoured with the attention of the House —
you did a fine thing; but don't spoil it, Clement,
my boy!

CLEMENT.

What do you mean ?   What is there to spoil ?

DICK.

Your career.   D'ye think I haven't seen this
coming on — your giving little Lavender hints in
grammar and composition, and buying her Boyle's
Arithmetic, and explaining the difference between
a Cape and an Isthmus in the dusk by that window ?   No, no, Clement, my boy, it wouldn't answer — for the sake of her peace of mind and your
future, pull up before the mischief's done !

CLEMENT.

[*Taking* DICK's *hand.*]   You're too late, Dick.
I love her.

DICK.

[*Spluttering with anger, and shaking his fist at*
CLEMENT.]   Out of my chambers !   This is gratitude.
This is how you profit by the counsel and companion-
ship of a man double your age !   I've done with you.

CLEMENT.

Very well, Dick.

DICK.

[*Rushing at him.*]   Clement, my boy, I'm a little
angry now — [*tearfully*] — but I shall work round,
Clem.   You haven't breathed a word to the poor
child, have you ?

CLEMENT.

Not a word, Dick.

DICK.

Thank you, Clem. Lavvy must be sent into the country for the benefit of her health, and then — there'll be an end of it.

CLEMENT.

Dick! Why should there be an end of it?

DICK.

Don't talk to me, sir, like that! Haven't you been adopted by a Mr. What's-his-name, a banker, sir?

CLEMENT.

Well?

DICK.

If a banker should adopt *me*, you'd see something like behaviour, sir. Why, if you offend your father, as you call him, you'll be a pauper; you'll be like Richard Phenyl, Esq., of the Inner Temple!

CLEMENT.

Why should I offend Mr. Wedderburn by loving a girl who is simple and honest and generous and courtly; whose only vice is that she is not dressed by a Bond Street milliner?

DICK.

Don't come to me when you're starving, that's all.

CLEMENT.

Nonsense, Dick. At the worst I shall have my profession.

DICK.

Profession ! What good is my profession to *me?*
[*Snatching a dirty pipe from the mantelpiece savagely.*] Besides, ain't you engaged to a beautiful —
a Miss Thing-a-my — Mr. Wedderburn's niece ?

CLEMENT.

Mrs. Gilfillian's daughter and I were thrown
together as children, and I believe there was some
idea —

DICK.

Ha ! You believe !

CLEMENT.

But I'm sure that Minnie Gilfillian troubles her
pretty head very little about me.

DICK.

Hadn't you better wait till Miss Gilfillian and
Mrs. Gilfillian and Mr. Wedderburn bring their
three pretty heads back to England ?

CLEMENT.

Wait ! I can't stop the beating of my heart, Dick
— and it beats Lavender, Lavender, Lavender, every
moment of the day. [*He buries his head in his hands.*

DICK.

One last word, Clement, my boy. [*Slowly and carefully filling his pipe.*] The story of Cinderella hasn't
been properly told yet. There was no pumpkin and
no fairy. The carriage came from Windover's and
the pair of bays from Tattersall's, at the young

gentleman's order.   The girl was pretty and good,
and he loved her, Clement, but the time arrived
when the slippers wore down at the heel and had
to be replaced by a size larger.   And, by and bye
— it's a sad story — he noticed that her little sharp
elbows didn't get whiter, poor thing ! and that she
mixed up the first and third person in accepting
Lady Montmorency's kind invitation to dine.   And
one day a carriage and pair were for sale, Clement
— as good as new — the property of a gentleman
leaving England, who was no longer answerable for
the debts contracted by Cinderella, his wife.

CLEMENT.

The hero of your story was a cad, Dick !

DICK.

The hero of any story generally is.   There — take
my sermon or leave it.   But it's because I love
you, and because this poor woman, Ruth Rolt, has
been for fifteen years a good friend to a shaggy
worthless cur, that I won't let you and her child
make each other wretched without raising my bark
against it.   Amen, Clement, my boy — Amen !

> [*He drops into the armchair facing the fire
> and lights his pipe.   There is a low
> knock from the other side of the cur-
> tained opening.*

CLEMENT.

There's that man of mine, Jenks — he gets later
and later every morning.

DICK.

[*Growling.*]　Learn to dress yourself.　*I* dress
myself.　　　　　　　　[*The knock is repeated.*

CLEMENT.

[*Angrily.*]　Come in!

LAVENDER, *a slight pretty girl, about seventeen,
shabbily dressed, draws the curtain and enters
the room.　Her voice is sweet and gentle, and her
movements graceful and refined.　She carries
some school-books, an "exercise" book, and a
small tray.*

LAVENDER.

[*Standing unnoticed — timidly.*]　May I clear
the table, please?

DICK.

[*Turning in his chair.*]　Hallo!

CLEMENT.

[*Jumping up.*]　Good gracious!　We thought
you were Jenks.

LAVENDER.

[*Taking a little crumpled note from her pocket.*]
Jenks has just left this note downstairs, Mr. Hale.

CLEMENT.

[*Reading.*]　" Henry Jenks presents his respect-
ful compliments, but I am not coming any more
has I — " H'm.　Hand that to Mr. Phenyl, Lavender.

[LAVENDER *gives the note to* DICK.

DICK.

[*Reading.*] "I am not coming any more has I can't stand the carryings on of that awful Mr. Phenyl." [*Indignantly.*] Well — I —

> [*He screws up the note vindictively and throws it into the fire ; then turning, he sees* LAVENDER *and* CLEMENT *close together.*

LAVENDER.

[*Giving the books to* CLEMENT, *reluctantly.*] You won't look at my exercise till I've cleared the breakfast table and gone right out of sight, will you ?

CLEMENT.

Why ?

LAVENDER.

It's so blotty.

DICK.

[*Fidgeting.*] H'm ! Clement, my boy ! [*Admonishing* CLEMENT *by waving his pipe.*]

> [LAVENDER *goes to the breakfast table and begins removing the things.*

CLEMENT.

[*Angrily.*] Don't interfere, Dick.

DICK.

Thank you, Mr. Hale. [*Stalking away indignantly.*

CLEMENT.

[*To himself.*] Confound Dick's cynicism. How

sweet she is. [*To* LAVENDER.] May I help in
some way ?   [*He takes up the teapot.*

LAVENDER.

No, thank you. [*Taking the teapot from* CLEM-
ENT *and looking at his empty plate.*] Poor Mr.
Phenyl hasn't eaten any breakfast.

CLEMENT.

Ah, poor Mr. Phenyl.

> [*She carries some of the breakfast things
> out into the passage and puts them on
> the butler's tray.* CLEMENT *hesitates a
> moment, then snatches up an egg-cup
> and goes after her.*

DICK.

[*Looking round.*] Where, where ? [*Going to
the curtained opening.*] Ah, Clement, my boy.

> [CLEMENT *returns to the room, glaring at*
> DICK, *and stands sulkily before the fire.*
> LAVENDER *goes on clearing the table.*
> DICK *throws himself on the sofa, opens
> the newspaper, and eyes* CLEMENT *and*
> LAVENDER *from behind it.*

CLEMENT.

Do you know that your books are to be closed,
Lavender ?

LAVENDER.

[*Starting.*] My books !

CLEMENT.

Pounds, shillings, and pence are to be withdrawn from your mental banking account; the intricate verb will torture you no longer ; and the mountains of this world will have to settle their relative height amongst themselves.

LAVENDER.

[*Falteringly.*] I was afraid I was becoming too troublesome to you, Mr. Hale.

CLEMENT.

My dear child, it's not my doing, but Doctor Delaney's.

LAVENDER.

Oh, how cruel ! He doesn't know how ignorant and stupid I am !
[*She returns to the passage in tears.*

CLEMENT.

[*Savagely to* DICK.] There !

DICK.

Think of your health, Lavvy. Health should be the first consideration with us all.

[LAVENDER *returns, wiping her eyes, to brush away the crumbs.*

CLEMENT.

But I've a capital notion. If you may not *read*, there's nothing to prevent your being *read to.*

DICK.

Eh ?

CLEMENT.

And so, Lavender, every evening for a couple of
hours I'll grind out some sound instructive work
and you shall sit and listen to me.

LAVENDER.

[*Gratefully.*]   Oh, Mr. Hale! how good you are !

CLEMENT.

I'll lay in a stock of books this morning.   We'll
begin on " Frederick the Great," by Carlyle.

DICK.

Twenty-one volumes !

> [LAVENDER *having cleared the table, now
> removes the white cloth and begins to
> fold it.*

CLEMENT.

[*Advancing.*]   Allow me ?

LAVENDER.

Thank you, Mr. Hale.

> [CLEMENT *takes an end of the tablecloth
> opposite* LAVENDER.   DICK *savagely
> screws the paper into a ball and flings
> it away.   There is a sharp rat-tat-tat
> at the outer door.*

DICK.

[*Taking* LAVENDER'S *end of the tablecloth from
her.*]   Go to the door, Lavvy.

[CLEMENT *folds the cloth angrily with*
DICK. LAVENDER *opens the door and
admits* HORACE BREAM, *a good-looking,
well-dressed fair-haired young American.*

HORACE.

[*At the door.*] Thank you — Mr. Hale ? Thank
you. [*Advancing and looking from* CLEMENT *to*
DICK.] You'll excuse me, I hope, but being rather
in a hurry — [*to* DICK] — Hale ?

DICK.

Dropping his end of the tablecloth.] No — Phenyl!

HORACE.

[*To* CLEMENT.] Mr. Hale, I am perfectly delighted
to make your acquaintance. Permit me to carry
this through with you.

[*Placing his hat and stick on the floor, he
picks up the end of the tablecloth and
folds it with* CLEMENT, *who glares at
him in annoyance.* DICK *sits on the
sofa, chuckling.* LAVENDER *is seen
from time to time in the passage taking
away the breakfast things.*

CLEMENT.

Really, I haven't the pleasure of —

HORACE.

Horace Pinkley Bream.

CLEMENT.

Well, but —

HORACE.

I have the honour to be a great personal friend of your aunt, Mrs. Gilfillian, and her daughter Minnie. [*Warmly.*] Sir, most charming ladies.

CLEMENT.

Oh, pray sit down.

HORACE.

[*Sitting.*] I'm in a very great hurry.

CLEMENT.

Have you any message from — ?

HORACE.

[*Unconcernedly.*] No, sir, I have not.

CLEMENT.

[*Commanding himself.*] Then would you mind telling me — ?

HORACE.

[*Looking at his watch.*] Certainly. The fact is, your party picked me up in Paris two months ago.

CLEMENT.

What party ?

HORACE.

Mr. Wedderburn, his sister, Mrs. Gilfillian, and her daughter. Sir, charming ladies ! From Paris we travelled to Marseilles ; from Marseilles to Cannes ; Cannes to Nice. They just stuck to me right through. [*Looking round.*] Sir, I am delighted with your apartments.

CLEMENT.

[*To himself.*] An intrusive *table d'hôte* acquaintance. [*To* HORACE.] You left my friends at Nice, I presume ?

HORACE.

No, sir; we are home.

CLEMENT.

Home !

HORACE.

I brought Mrs. Gilfillian and her daughter right through to London yesterday. Charming ladies.

DICK.

[*To himself.*] Hallo !

CLEMENT.

[*Under his breath.*] Confound it !

HORACE.

We left Wedderburn in Paris, buying things. An exceedingly pleasant gentleman.

CLEMENT.

[*Distractedly.*] And where are Mrs. Gilfillian and her daughter now ?

HORACE.

That's my difficulty — where ? I lost 'em at Charing Cross station last night. Having heard them frequently talk about you, I dug up your old apartments in Pear Tree Court, where I found your notice of removal. You have not seen Mrs. Gilfillian yet ?

CLEMENT.

No, sir.

HORACE.

Thank you ; good morning. [*Presenting a card to* CLEMENT.] You have not been on our side, probably ?

CLEMENT.

No.

HORACE.

Sir, you'll just love N'York. [*Shaking hands with* CLEMENT *warmly.*] I regret that I am rather in a hurry. [*Handing a card to* DICK, *and shaking hands.*] Sir, good morning. You'll hear from me the very moment I've discovered these charming ladies.

CLEMENT.

But pardon my putting it so plainly, perhaps they don't want you to discover them.

HORACE.

[*Looking at his watch.*] Sorry I can't discuss that question just now. I'm rather in a hurry.

[*He goes out quickly.*

DICK.

Clement, my boy ! Mrs. Gilfillian and her daughter are in London ! The hand of Fate !

CLEMENT.

[*With determination.*] I shall be happy to see them, Dick, and to shake the hand of Fate. If I'm not in when they call, say I'll be back in half-an-hour.

DICK.

1 don't like your look, Clem. What are you going to do ?

CLEMENT.

Do, Dick ! I am going out to buy " Frederick the Great," by Carlyle.

[*He goes into his bedroom.* LAVENDER *appears in the passage.*

DICK.

[*Calling after* CLEMENT.] Leave my chambers to-day ! I've done with you ! [*To himself.*] If Ruth could only afford to send little Lavvy away for the benefit of her health, what a solution it would be. I think I could contrive it if I had a few pounds to spare. But if I had a few pounds to spare, I couldn't spare 'em. Lavender ! [LAVENDER *takes the folded tablecloth from the table and puts it away in the side-board.*] [*Thinking.*] Cripps has a fellow reading with him who wants to buy a little library. [*Looking towards the bookshelves.*] There's my little library ; the last remainder of the time when, if Cripps's pupil is good for fifteen pounds, I'll lend 'em to Ruth Rolt, and Lavvy shall leave town. [*Eyeing* LAVENDER.] Brighton into fifteen quid won't go. Broadstairs into fifteen quid, four weeks and one day over. [*Shaking his fist at the books.*] Come on ! [*Taking down the books, savagely.*] I'll teach you to remind me of the time when I was a promising lad like Cripps's pupil !

LAVENDER.

[*Watching him in surprise.*] May I help you, Mr. Phenyl ?

[DICK *drops a book and looks guiltily at* LAVENDER.

DICK.

For sale, Lavvy — library of Richard Phenyl, Esquire, of the Inner Temple, Barrister-at-law — fifty volumes.

LAVENDER.

[*Sympathetically.*] Oh! [*Laying her hand on his arm.*] *Must* you?

DICK.

[*Hesitatingly.*] Well — I — [*Looking at* LAVENDER, *then towards* CLEMENT'S *door — stroking her hair.*] I think I'd better, Lavvy.

LAVENDER.

Poor Mr. Phenyl! Shall I hand you the books?

DICK.

[*To himself.*] She makes me feel guilty. [*Tenderly.*] Lavvy, if your mother could afford it, would you like three or four weeks in the country?

LAVENDER.

Oh, no!

DICK.

[*Sharply.*] No?

[*She hands him volume after volume, from the bookcase; after looking at the titlepages he throws them on to the floor.*

LAVENDER.

The temple *is* the country — we have trees and grass, and birds and flowers.

DICK.

Seaside, then ?

LAVENDER.

No, we have a river with boats on it.

DICK.

Pooh, Lavvy! Think of fresh air, fresh eggs, fresh milk from the cow. We are all apt to underrate the importance of milk from the cow.

LAVENDER.

No. I'm happy here — so happy!

DICK.

[*To himself.*] Thinking of *him !* — Thinking of *him !*

LAVENDER.

Why do you look at the title-pages ?

DICK.

I'm sorting my property from the other young gentleman's, Mr. Hale's.

LAVENDER.

[*Eagerly.*] Oh, let me do it ! I'll look for Mr. Hale's name ! I'll take care you don't sell any of his. May I ?

DICK.

Very well, Lavvy.

[*She takes a quantity of books from the shelves, places them on the ground and kneels amongst them.*

DICK.

[*To himself.*] It's like setting her to sign her own death-warrant. Cripps is in court to-day in the Baxter case; I'll run over and see him. [*He goes quickly to the outer door, opens it, then returns, leaving the door slightly open.*] Going out without dressing! I'm upset — feel I'm doing a mean thing. [*Looking towards* LAVENDER — *tearfully.*] Poor Clem — poor Lavvy!

> [*He goes into his bedroom.* LAVENDER *examines the books and makes a neat pile of them as she hums a song happily.* CLEMENT, *fashionably dressed for walking, enters, unheard by* LAVENDER, *and watches her.*

CLEMENT.

[*To himself.*] She makes a room seem like a garden.

LAVENDER.

[*Taking up a book.*] "Smith's Leading Cases." [*Opening it.*] Looks rather dry — no conversation.
> [*She puts it aside.*

CLEMENT.

[*To himself.*] Why should I hold my tongue?

> [*He silently draws the curtain over the opening, without noticing that the door leading on to the outer passage is open.*

LAVENDER.

[*Taking up another book.*] "Benjamin on Sales." Biblical. Richard Phenyl.

[CLEMENT *goes to* DICK's *door, listens, and then quietly turns the key.*

LAVENDER.

[*With another book.*] "Williams on the Law of Real Property." Clement Hale. Ah! [*She opens the middle of the book.*] "Incorporeal Heredita-ments." What a beautiful book!

[*She settles herself a little nearer the window and reads earnestly.* CLEMENT *comes and sits upon the pile of books beside her.*

CLEMENT.

[*Softly.*] Lavender.
[*With a low cry of fright she turns slowly and looks at him.*

LAVENDER.

What are you doing there, Mr. Hale?

CLEMENT.

I've come to sit with you in the garden.

LAVENDER.

The garden!
[*Staring at him, she tries to rise ; he stretches out his hand and takes hers.*

LAVENDER.

[*Under her breath.*] Mr. Hale!

CLEMENT.

[*Drawing her down near him, and looking into her face earnestly.*] I love you Lavender, with all my heart. Will you be my wife?

[*She shrinks away, still staring at him.*

CLEMENT.

Speak to me. You don't mean no!

LAVENDER.

[*Faintly.*] I don't know what I mean.

CLEMENT.

[*Tenderly.*] Think about it. Think about it — here.

[*He gently draws her to him and clasps her in his arms.*

LAVENDER.

[*Half crying.*] You — you oughtn't to love *me!*

CLEMENT.

Why?

LAVENDER.

You know, I'm not — a lady.

CLEMENT.

My dear Princess.

LAVENDER.

I work. Ah, how red my hands are!

CLEMENT.

Because your blushes run down into them. When you're accustomed to being my wife, they'll grow quite white.

LAVENDER.

But look at me — my frocks can't keep secrets if I can; I'm very poor.

CLEMENT.

I'll be poor with you, if it comes to that.

LAVENDER.

[*Looking up into his face.*]   Are you poor?

CLEMENT.

I've nothing — of my own — but my profession. [*Thoughtfully.*]   I may become very poor.

LAVENDER.

[*Rising quickly.*]   Oh!

CLEMENT.

[*Retreating a little.*]   Do you like me less for that?

LAVENDER.

[*Going towards him.*]   Less!   [*Checking herself.*] I — I haven't said I like you at all, but if I ever did like you, it would be because I know *how* to be poor, and could teach you the way to bear it.

CLEMENT.

[*Drawing her to him.*]   My sweet, sweet Lavender!

LAVENDER.

[*In a whisper.*]   Clement.   You know how pale
I've been looking lately.

CLEMENT.

Yes ! that's why I asked Delaney to call.

LAVENDER.

Foolish boy !   I shall have red cheeks to-morrow.
I — I've been thinking so much about you, Clement.

CLEMENT.

[*Laughing.*]   Lavender !

LAVENDER.

Ah, don't laugh at me !

> [*She sits upon the sofa, hiding her face. He
> goes to her and kneels by her side.*

CLEMENT.

Why were you sitting amongst those books ?

LAVENDER.

Mr. Phenyl is obliged to sell them.

CLEMENT.

He sha'n't do anything of the kind.   We'll stick
to old Dick, won't we ?

LAVENDER.

Always.   And we won't let mother work any
more, will we ?

CLEMENT.

Never.

LAVENDER.

[*Happily.*]   Ah!

CLEMENT.

Tell me again you love me.

LAVENDER.

I never will.   You make me say things and then you laugh at me.   [*Bending her head to his.*]   I love you.

The curtain over the doorway is pushed aside, and
MRS. GILFILLIAN *enters followed by* MINNIE.
MRS. GILFILLIAN *is a sedate aristocratic-looking
woman about fifty, with a lofty forehead and
side curls.* MINNIE *is a handsome, lively young
woman.   Both are fashionably dressed.   On discovering* CLEMENT *at* LAVENDER'S *feet* MRS.
GILFILLIAN *clutches* MINNIE *by the arm, and
takes her out;* CLEMENT *and* LAVENDER *with
their heads close together being unconscious of
interruption.   There is then a loud rat-tat-tat
at the outer door.* CLEMENT *and* LAVENDER
*rise quickly, she dropping among the books,
while he goes and draws the curtain and discov-
ers* MRS. GILFILLIAN *and* MINNIE.

CLEMENT.

My dear aunt.

MRS. GILFILLIAN *enters the room followed by* MINNIE.

MRS. GILFILLIAN.

[*Much disturbed, giving* CLEMENT *two fingers.*]

We found your door open, Clement, but I preferred knocking.

CLEMENT.

[*Unhappily.*]   Delighted, aunt.

    [MRS. GILFILLIAN *walks straight across to* LAVENDER, *looking down upon her through her pince-nez.*

CLEMENT.

[*To* MINNIE.]   Minnie.

MINNIE.

[*Demurely.*]   Well, Clem.

CLEMENT.

[*Hesitatingly.*]   This is a jolly surprise.

MINNIE.

[*Looking at* LAVENDER.]   'M — yes.

    [LAVENDER *having pushed the books out of the way, goes out of the room,* MRS. GIL-FILLIAN *looking after her.* MINNIE *takes up one of the books, looking at it inquisitively.*

CLEMENT.

Those are the books we slave at, Minnie.

MINNIE.

[*Glancing at him shyly.*]   Don't you overdo it, Clem.

MRS. GILFILLIAN.

[*Looking after* LAVENDER.] That's a wicked young woman!

[*She shuts the door, and joins* CLEMENT, *as* MINNIE *looks round the room.*

MRS. GILFILLIAN.

We left Nice on Tuesday, Clement. Minnie and I came straight through, but Mr. Wedderburn prefers to dawdle for a week in Paris. [*Handing* CLEMENT *a packet of cabinet photographs.*] He sends you those portraits, done by Grotz of Monte Carlo. [*Nervously.*] Minnie, don't pry.

CLEMENT.

[*Looking at the photographs.*] Dear old guv'nor! [*Reading the superscription on one of the portraits.*] "For my boy — from Geoffrey Wedderburn." [*To* MRS. GILFILLIAN.] The fact is, aunt, I've already heard of your return from a gentleman who was good enough to call on me.

MRS. GILFILLIAN.

Not Mr. Bream!

CLEMENT.

Horace Pinkley Bream!

MRS. GILFILLIAN.

[*Sinking into armchair.*] Oh!

MINNIE.

[*Sitting on sofa.*] Oh, ma!

Mrs. Gilfillian.

We shall never shake him off.   He saved Minnie's
life in Paris by pulling her from under a tramcar
in the Avenue Mirabeau.

Clement.

Good gracious !

Mrs. Gilfillian.

So careless of her to get there !   I closed my
eyes and in imagination heard the cracking of her
bones.   This person rushed forward and restored
her to the side-walk, as he will persist in calling the
pavement.

Clement.

I should like to thank him.

Mrs. Gilfillian.

Don't !   He'll never leave you if you do.   I
thanked him — although he's not at all the young
man I would have selected to rescue a child of mine.

Clement.

[*Uneasily.*]   In London for long, aunt ?

Mrs. Gilfillian.

The season.   We have rooms at the Metropole,
but we shall eat at these new coffee establishments
in Regent Street.   Oh, will you oblige me by taking a shilling cab to the hotel, and asking my maid,
Bodly, for my vinaigrette ?

Clement.

Certainly.

[*He lays the photographs on the table and
takes up his hat and umbrella.*

MRS. GILFILLIAN.

You lunch here ?

CLEMENT.

It's sent in at one o'clock.

MRS. GILFILLIAN.

We could remain, if —

CLEMENT.

[*Blankly.*] Delighted.

MRS. GILFILLIAN.

[*To herself.*] He must never be left again.

CLEMENT.

[*Banging his hat on his head.*] Confound !

    [*He goes out.* MRS. GILFILLIAN *looks to
    see that the door is closed, then rises, and
    crosses to* MINNIE.

MRS. GILFILLIAN.

[*With a gasp.*] Minnie, my poor child ! You
saw that young woman ?

MINNIE.

I'm afraid I did, mamma.

MRS. GILFILLIAN.

What were they doing ? I have never felt my
near sight so keenly.

MINNIE.

Clement was kneeling, mamma — in an ordinary
way. And I think he was holding her hand.

MRS. GILFILLIAN.

Ah, I saw that!

MINNIE.

And she was looking down — in an ordinary way.

MRS. GILFILLIAN.

[*Pacing to and fro.*] In the very room in which we are asked to take luncheon.

MINNIE.   ·

Don't be cross, ma, dear. She is very pretty and innocent-looking.

MRS. GILFILLIAN.

Innocent-looking! Do you think I will have my plans — my plans and my brother's — frustrated by a girl with ulterior motives and eyes like saucers?

MINNIE.

Look here, ma, darling. Clement is grown up now and may do just as he pleases. I am quite fond of Clem, always was, and if he asked me to be his wife — well, I should want to know all about that young woman. But I don't care a pin for Uncle Geoffrey's plans, and if Clem doesn't take to me — as I'm sure he ought to — why, bless him, I'll be his wife's bridesmaid and her friend into the bargain.

MRS. GILFILLIAN.

[*Indignantly.*] Minnie! [*Suddenly.*] Hush!

[*The handle of the door of* DICK'S *room is rattled from the inside.*

MRS. GILFILLIAN.

[*With horror.*] Minnie! There's somebody else in that room!

MINNIE.

[*Retreating.*] Oh, ma!

MRS. GILFILLIAN.

And *this* is the Law!

DICK.

[*From within.*] Clement! Clement!

MRS. GILFILLIAN.

[*Listening.*] It's a man's voice — *or a deep contralto.*

DICK.

[*Still within.*] Locked in, Clement, my boy.

[MRS. GILFILLIAN *turns the key in the door, and retreats.* DICK *enters in the old and worn wig and gown of a barrister.*

DICK.

Thank you. [*Enquiringly.*] To see Mr. Hale?

MRS. GILFILLIAN.

Oh, I have *seen* Mr. Hale. May I ask —?

DICK.

Richard Phenyl. Hale and I live together.

MRS. GILFILLIAN.

[*Eagerly.*] Dear me! I wish to speak to you

immediately. Mrs. Gilfillian. [*Introducing* MIN-
NIE.] My daughter.

> [MINNIE *laughs behind her handkerchief
> at* DICK'S *appearance.*

DICK.

[*Politely.*] Heard of you.

MRS. GILFILLIAN.

[*Quietly to* MINNIE.] Go away. Go away ! Perhaps this gentleman will allow you to try the piano.
[MINNIE, *with a toss of the head goes to the piano.*]
[*To* DICK.] Mr. Funnel, I have just received a
great shock.   [MINNIE *plays a sentimental air.*

MRS. GILFILLIAN.

Who is the young woman who frequents these
rooms ?

DICK.

Young woman ?

MRS. GILFILLIAN.

We came in suddenly. A girl was seated on that
sofa. Ugh ! Clement was on his *knees* before her,
Mr. Funnel.

DICK.

[*To himself.*] He's done it ! He's done it !

MRS. GILFILLIAN.

Minnie got me away somehow, unheard by either

of them! But my poor child. Mr. Funnel—[*tear-fully*]—the blow has fallen there.

> [MINNIE *strikes in suddenly with a very lively air.*

MRS. GILFILLIAN.

· Minnie!

> [MINNIE *stops playing, and* MRS. GILFILLIAN *goes to her remonstrating.*

DICK.

[*To himself.*] We're in for it. We've made our choice. We prefer linsey and a linen collar to satin and *Valenciennes.* Very well! Now it's come to it, I'll stick to you, Clement, my boy! [*Arranging his wig and gown, and striking a forensic attitude.*] For the defendant!

MRS. GILFILLIAN.

[*Returning to* DICK.] What you tell me is in perfect confidence.

DICK.

Not at all necessary, m'm—we court inquiry. The young lady is the daughter of Mrs. Rolt, who resides, to put it plainly, in the basement.

MRS. GILFILLIAN.

A low woman?

DICK.

[*Pointing downwards.*] Geographically — not otherwise.   [MINNIE *resumes playing softly.*

MRS. GILFILLIAN.

Nonsense, sir. These people attend upon you. This girl's mother is what you call a common servant.

DICK.

No, ma'am — she is what I call a lady.

' MRS. GILFILLIAN.

A lady ?

DICK.

Madam, Mrs. Rolt has been a kind, faithful friend to me for fifteen years. If I have the privilege of knowing you for that length of time nothing will induce me to speak ill of you.

RUTH *enters, and stands in the opening to passage.*

MRS. GILFILLIAN.

I'll see Mrs. Rolt at once. Kindly ring the bell.

[DICK *moves towards the bell-handle and sees* RUTH.

DICK.

Here is Mrs. Rolt.

RUTH.

[*Announcing.*] Mr. Bream, please.

HORACE *enters quickly ;* DICK *speaks to* RUTH.

HORACE.

[*With outstretched hands.*] My dear Mrs. Gilfillian ! [MINNIE *stops playing suddenly, and rises.*

MINNIE.

Oh!

MRS. GILFILLIAN.

[*In consternation.*]   Mr. Bream!

HORACE.

[*Excitedly.*] Lost you at the Custom House counter last night — saw you in a hansom this morning — never meant to rest till I'd found you.

[HORACE *goes to* MINNIE.

MRS. GILFILLIAN.

[*Helplessly sinking into a chair.*] Oh, dear me!

HORACE.

[*To* MINNIE, *taking her hand.*] My dear Miss Gilfillian!

MINNIE.

[*Distractedly.*] Oh, how do you do, Mr. Bream?

RUTH.

[*Quietly to* MRS. GILFILLIAN.] You wish to speak to me, ma'am?

MRS. GILFILLIAN.

[*Rising.*] Mrs. Rolt!

RUTH.

Yes.

MRS. GILFILLIAN.

I have discovered that there have been — some — love passages between Mr. Hale and your daughter. I — I —

RUTH.

Yes. My daughter has just told me that Mr. Hale has offered her marriage.

MRS. GILFILLIAN.

Marriage. [*Checking herself.*] Don't you understand that this is a terrible shock to Mr. Hale's friends?

RUTH.

[*Tearfully.*] I understand that it is a terrible shock to me to lose my child. ·

[RUTH *turns away, and leans faintly on the back of a chair.*

MRS. GILFILLIAN.

To lose your child. I see. [*To herself.*] It's serious; I'll telegraph at once to brother Geoffrey.

[MRS. GILFILLIAN *seats herself at writing table and begins writing rapidly.* RUTH'S *eye falls upon the photographs lying on table; she stares at them for a moment blankly.*

RUTH.

[*Commanding herself — going a step or two towards* DICK.] Mr. Phenyl. [*Pointing to the photograph.*] Who,— who is that?

DICK.

Mr. Wedderburn, I think.

RUTH.

[*With a start.*] Wedderburn!

DICK.

Banker at Barnchester — Mr. Hale is his adopted son.

RUTH.

In — indeed. [*After a pause she goes quickly to* MRS. GILFILLIAN, *and whispers.*] Madam! Madam! [MRS. GILFILLIAN *turns.*] You — you have misunderstood me. I — I give you my word my daughter shall never marry Mr. Hale.

MRS. GILFILLIAN.

[*Rising, with the written telegram in her hand.*] ˙ What!

RUTH.

[*Glancing round.*] Hush!

      [LAVENDER *enters the passage, and takes up the tray from the butler's stand.* CLEMENT *follows and stands whispering to her.* MINNIE *and* HORACE *are in close conversation.*

END OF THE FIRST ACT.

The scene is the same as in the first act. A day has passed and it is now evening.

DICK, *looking somewhat neater than before, is sitting in an armchair, smoking his pipe thoughtfully.* RUTH *enters quietly, carrying a tray with tea-things, and a letter.*

RUTH.

A cab has just brought this letter for Mr. Hale. I'll place it here.

[*She lays the letter on one of the teacups; DICK rises and intercepts her as she is going out.*

DICK.

How's Lavvy to-night — any better?

RUTH.

[*Tremblingly.*] N — no — No better.

CLEMENT, *in walking dress, and carrying a handsome basket of flowers, enters hurriedly.*

60

CLEMENT.

Any good news, Dick ?

DICK.

[*With a grunt.*] No.

[DICK *walks to and fro moodily.*

CLEMENT.

How is she, Mrs. Rolt ?

RUTH.

I fear just the same.

CLEMENT.

May I not see her for a moment — call to her at her door ? I'll be quiet enough.

RUTH.

No, no — not yet.

CLEMENT.

Not yet, Mrs. Rolt. Still not yet. Oh, you mothers !

RUTH.

[*Bitterly.*] Oh — we mothers !

CLEMENT.

[*Handing her the basket of flowers.*] Give her these flowers with my — Say I — You know.

[*He drops disconsolately into the armchair.*

RUTH.

[*Calmly.*] Thank you. They are very beautiful.

[*She goes out;* CLEMENT *then rises impatiently.*

CLEMENT.

Dick, Dick!

DICK.

Clement!

CLEMENT.

The idea tortures me that something is being
kept from us! By Mrs. Rolt's manner there's a
mystery, Dick!

DICK.

You're right, Clement, my boy. By some inde-
finable instinct I feel we are being *done*, sir!

[DICK *hurls his pipe furiously into the grate,
and sits in the armchair.*

CLEMENT.

Lavender loves me — I'll never doubt that.

DICK.

Oh, she loves us right enough — we needn't dis-
tress ourselves on that score.

CLEMENT.

But this illness! "I shall have red cheeks to-
morrow," she said, Dick — meaning that she was
well and happy; and then, an hour afterwards —
ill! Too ill to be seen, too ill to send me a word
of comfort. Last night — worse. This morning —
worse. To-night — no better. Dick, it's unendur-
able.

DICK.

[*Rising with judicial solemnity, and warming
himself by the fire.*] Well, you know, Clement,

my boy, we *may* be unduly distressing ourselves —
I say *ourselves,* because iu this case Mr. Richard
Phenyl is *with* you.

CLEMENT.

Bless you, Dick !

DICK.

We should remember that we are youngsters at
this sort of game ; that this is, in point of fact, the
first time we have offered ourselves in marriage.
For all we know, the prospect of an alliance with
us would set up a condition of cerebral excitement
in *any* young lady. [*Taking up the poker to aid
him in his argument.*] No, no, Clement, my boy,
it isn't Lavvy's illness that puzzles me —

CLEMENT.

What then, Dick ?

DICK.

Why, the sudden, self-satisfied affability of our
aunt, Mrs. Gilfillian.

CLEMENT.

Ah! .

DICK.

[*Flourishing the poker.*] There's an unpleasant
air of truculent triumph in our aunt's demeanour
that I resent, Clement, my boy !

CLEMENT.

And I too, Dick ! And the incessant civility
and attention I'm in duty bound to show Mrs.
Gilfillian drives me mad. Good gracious, Dick !
she and Minnie never leave me for a moment !

DICK.

Our aunt is undoubtedly a barnacle, Clement, my boy.

CLEMENT.

They lunched here yesterday — you know.

DICK.

I know.

CLEMENT.

Afterwards dragging me to the Park for two hours in a ridiculous hired landau, and ending by carrying me off to a classical concert in the evening.

DICK.

I feel for you, Clement, though I was at a smoking concert myself last night.

CLEMENT.

This morning, didn't they breakfast with us ?

DICK.

Our forthcoming weekly bill will testify that they *did !*

CLEMENT.

Then we went shopping in Bond Street, asked the price of everything, and had little cold veal pies for luncheon at a ladies' confectioners.

DICK.

[*With a wry face.*]   Oh, don't, Clem, don't !

CLEMENT.

After that we visited picture galleries, till I lost all patience, declared I was neglecting my studies and rushed away to buy a few flowers for my dear one.

DICK.

Well, Clem, perhaps it enables you to forget for a minute or two the poor little sick girl downstairs.

CLEMENT.

Ah, Dick, that's unworthy of you! Why, every street to me is "Lavender Street;" the newsboys shout nothing but "Lavender!" "Evening Lavender!" and the flower girls sell only sweet Lavender from their baskets. The whole world is perfumed with Lavender; and yet she and I seem so far apart. Dick — so very far apart.

[*There is a rat-tat at the outer door.*

DICK.

A visitor. Can it be our aunt?

CLEMENT.

[*Wearily.*] Open the door, Dick, like a good fellow.

[DICK *opens the door,* MINNIE *is outside.*

DICK.

Miss Gilfillian!

MINNIE.

Yes. May I see Clement, Mr. Phenyl?

DICK.

I don't wish to dazzle you, Miss Gilfillian, but you may see *both* of us. Come in.

MINNIE *enters.   She is handsomely dressed for the theatre.*

CLEMENT.

Why, Minnie!   Are you alone?

MINNIE.

Don't scold me, Clem.   [*Quietly to him.*]   I've something I must say to you in secret.

CLEMENT.

But where's aunt?

MINNIE.

[*Laughing.*]   I've given poor mamma what we children used to call the slip.

DICK.

Ah!   [*With a chuckle.*]   Ha! ha!   [MINNIE *turns to* DICK, *he pokes the fire.*]   I beg your pardon.

[CLEMENT *assists* MINNIE *to take off her cloak.*

MINNIE.

I'm afraid you're dreadfully shocked, Mr. Phenyl.

DICK.

No — no.

MINNIE.

While mamma was dressing for the theatre I stole away in a hansom.   I've left a note for her on my table.   [*Laughing.*]   Ha, ha!

DICK.

[*Joining in the laugh.*] Ha, ha!

MINNIE.

[*Suddenly serious.*] It's awfully wrong.

DICK.

[*Seriously.*] Yes, it'll vex our aunt — Mrs. Gilfillian.

MINNIE.

[*To* CLEMENT.] But mamma will call for us here at half-past eight, Clem dear.

CLEMENT.

For *us?*

MINNIE.

Why, haven't you received her letter?

DICK.

Dear me, quite forgot — letter for you somewhere, Clem. [*Arranging the armchair for* MINNIE.] Miss Gilfillian, toss for the armchair. I mean, try the armchair.

> [CLEMENT *finds the letter on the teacup and opens it.*

CLEMENT.

[*Reading the letter disconsolately.*] "We have a box for four persons for the Cabinet Theatre to witness the new play about which people talk so much — 'The Sealskin Jacket.' I hear it described as a salutary lesson to young men. We shall fetch you at half-past eight." [*Quietly to* Dick.]   Dick! I'm getting desperate!

DICK.

[*Under his breath, grasping* Clement's *hand.*] Bear up.   We must continue to hold a candle to — to aunt.

CLEMENT.

Why shouldn't you join us, and help me through the evening?   The box holds four.

DICK.

I know.   Our aunt spread out in front and the rest looking at her hair-pins.   No.

CLEMENT.

Dick, you're unkind.

DICK.

Unkind!   [*In a whisper.*]   Clement, my boy, have you *seen* my evening clothes?

CLEMENT.

No, Dick.

DICK.

Thought not.   The coat and waistcoat are in fair preservation, but the rest of it has been attending funerals for years.

MINNIE.

[*Tapping her foot impatiently.*]   Clement!

CLEMENT.

I beg your pardon, Minnie.

[MINNIE *eyes* DICK, *and looks at* CLEMENT *significantly.*

MINNIE.

[*In an undertone.*] Clement — Mr. Phenyl!

CLEMENT.

Oh! yes. [*Trying to attract* DICK'*s attention.*] Dick!

DICK.

[*Sitting at table.*] No, no.

CLEMENT.

Dick!

DICK.

Rather busy to-night, Clement, my boy.

[CLEMENT *makes signs to* DICK *to depart, while* DICK, *thinking that* CLEMENT *is renewing his persuasions with regard to the theatre, shakes his head.*

CLEMENT.

[*Impatiently.*] Dick! [*Whispers to him.*

DICK.

Oh! [*Shaking* CLEMENT'*s hand.*] My dear Clement!

[*He snatches up a book from the sofa, a newspaper from the table, and a pipe and tobacco jar from the mantelpiece, and goes to the door of his own room.*

DICK.

[*Innocently.*] Can you spare me for ten minutes, Clement ?

CLEMENT.

Certainly, Dick.

DICK.

Thank you.

[*He goes into his room.* MINNIE *watches to see the door close, then lays her hand upon* CLEMENT'S *arm.*

MINNIE.

[*Softly.*] Clem, dear, I've come to see you alone because I must put myself right with you.

CLEMENT.

Isn't it I who should put myself right with you, Minnie ?

MINNIE.

Don't be polite, Clem; and unless you tell me you hate me I shall cease to respect you.

CLEMENT.

Hate you !

MINNIE.

Why, look how mamma and I torture you all day by carrying you about with us ! Aren't you in agony, sir, the whole time ? What do you think you looked like this afternoon in Macnab's picture gallery in the Haymarket ?

CLEMENT.

I — I was so horribly anxious, Minnie, about —

MINNIE.

About your studies. Come, Clem. [*She takes
his hand and places him on the sofa, then sits on the
head of the sofa looking down upon him.*] Let us
be fogies for a moment. You know we were very
fond of each other as children, weren't we ?

CLEMENT.

Yes, Minnie, and —

MINNIE.

Hush ! Well, then, dear, as we grew up we grew
out of our love, as boys and girls outgrow their
clothes. Your love, as it were, got too short in
the waist, and mine wouldn't meet at the buttons.
And, at last, one fine day we yawned, Clem, and
the seams of our affection collapsed.

CLEMENT.

[*Taking her hand, embarrassed.*] My dear
Minnie —

MINNIE.

[*Sitting beside him.*] Ah, Clem, don't let us
mourn for it; we're lucky to have yawned in time,
dear. And so I want you to understand that I
won't help to mend and patch an old attachment;
I won't put an extra flounce or a new set of hooks
and eyes on a garment a couple of children wore to
rags years ago. There ! That's what I call putting
myself right with you.

CLEMENT.

[*Tenderly — taking her hands.*] My dear sister,
how compassionate you are to me !

MINNIE.

[*Smiling.*] And so you were on with the new love before you were off with the old — you bad boy !

CLEMENT.

I — I can't help loving her, Minnie.

MINNIE.

And you're quite sure there's plenty of devotion turned up at the edge, in case you haven't done growing ?

CLEMENT.

Ah, Minnie, I'm not so bad as that !

MINNIE.

I've no faith in you — monster. But, Clem, I'm dreadfully afraid mamma still thinks we shall make a match of it. [*Laughingly.*] Whenever mamma is triumphant her curls are always rigid, and to-day they're like little telescopes.

CLEMENT.

[*Angrily.*] Whatever happens, Minnie, I resent aunt's interference. I am a man now !

MINNIE.

Oh, yes, anybody can see that by the way you jilt people. But, Clem, dear, I wish you'd do something to please me.

CLEMENT.

I'll do anything !

MINNIE.

Anything but marry me. Well, don't wait for Uncle Geoffrey's return, but write to him to the Hotel Rivoli in Paris, and tell him how you adore — my hated rival. Uncle Geof. is a bachelor, but married men and bachelors are manufactured by the same process — love, Clem — and he'll understand. Tell him all, and say that the girl you have lost your treacherous heart to has won one staunch friend — Minnie Gilfillian.

CLEMENT.

My dear sister, I'll write directly I get back from the theatre. [*Putting his hand to his breast.*] Shall I send him her portrait ?

MINNIE.

[*Pointing.*] You've got one there !

CLEMENT.

How did you guess ?

MINNIE.

You silly boy ? Show it me.

> [*She sits in the armchair; he takes a small photograph from his pocket and hands it to her.*

MINNIE.

[*Leaning back scrutinising the portrait with a great air of indifference.*] So this is the little lady I saw yesterday, in her best frock, is it ?

CLEMENT.

Yes, I stole it from Dick Phenyl's album.

MINNIE.

A thief as well as a heart-breaker.   And you consider her really pretty ?

CLEMENT.

Say what you think, Minnie — I don't mind.

MINNIE.

Why she has only two eyes, as I have; and one nose and mouth just like me.   Now, I wonder why you jilted me for Lavender ?

CLEMENT.

You're only teasing me, aren't you ?

MINNIE.

Oh ! I don't condescend to tease bad men.   And what a very *little* girl she is.   I see, it's economy ; when you're married you'll only keep a goat chaise. [*Returning the photo.*] She can't weigh much, Clem.

CLEMENT.

Less than my heart does to-night, Minnie.   She is ill — suffering.

MINNIE.

[*Compassionately.*] Poor boy ! She'll be well to-morrow.

CLEMENT.

If anything happened to part us, Minnie! If I lost her !

MINNIE.

Hush, Clem !   [*Taking his hand.*]   I'll tell you.

When a girl knows she is loved by the man she loves she has a charmed life — her heart *can't* stop. If ever the *elixir vitæ* is discovered, Clem, it'll turn out to be a bottle of something to keep a man and a woman in love with each other. There, run along and put its pretty things on for the theatre !

[*He kisses her hand, and goes into his bedroom.*

MINNIE.

[*Seeing the tea-things.*] Tea ! [*Putting her hand on the teapot.*] Hot ! I must take to tea violently, now I'm going to be an old maid. To-morrow I'll buy a kitten. [*There is a rat-tat at the outer door.*] Mamma ! What a scolding's in store for me ! Oh, dear !

[*She goes to the door and opens it.* HORACE BREAM *is outside ; he is in evening dress, and carries a cane.*

HORACE.

Mr. Hale ?

MINNIE.

[*Startled.*] Oh ! [*She leaves the door in a flutter.*] Horace Bream ! How awkward !

[HORACE *closes the door and follows her into the room.*

HORACE.

My dear Miss Gilfillian !

MINNIE.

[*Uneasily.*] I daresay you're surprised —

meet — me — here. I — have missed mamma — somehow. Perhaps you will call again.

HORACE.

Very likely. If you remember I was here yesterday.

MINNIE.

[*Embarrassed.*] I mean, Mr. Hale may be quite ten minutes.

HORACE.

I shall be perfectly charmed if he's twenty.

MINNIE.

[*Coldly.*] If you decide to wait, Mr. Hale would like you to sit down, I'm sure.

HORACE.

[*Bowing.*] I'm sure he would.

MINNIE.

[*Pointing to a chair.*] D — don't mind me, please. [*She turns away abruptly, and sits at writing-table with her back towards* HORACE. *To herself.*] A man's the last creature to recognise the possibility of his being *de trop.*

HORACE.

[*Moodily, to himself, as he sits on the arm of the armchair.*] Well, the formality of an unmarried lady in England is perfectly chilling.

MINNIE.

[*To herself.*] What *does* he think of my being here.

HORACE.

[*To himself.*] I can't — I can't endure this a minute longer.

[*He crosses to the sofa, where he sits watching* MINNIE.

MINNIE.

[*To herself.*] How embarrassing! I wish I was buried!

HORACE.

[*To himself.*] If this continues for another five seconds I shall shriek aloud.

MINNIE.

I'll put a bold face on the matter — an American girl would be equal to twice this. [*Looking angrily at the back of the armchair, in which she supposes* HORACE *to be, while he watches her with curiosity.*] Bother! [HORACE *rises in surprise, and* MINNIE, *peeping over the back of the chair, finds it empty and turns, facing* HORACE *with a gasp.*] Oh! [*In confusion.*] Pray excuse my having left you for a moment. Will you have some tea?   [*Sitting.*

HORACE.

[*Resuming his seat.*] I shall be perfectly delighted. [*To himself.*] In English society while there is tea there is hope.

MINNIE.

Sugar?

HORACE.

Thank you. [*Cheerfully to himself.*] We have fairly started.

MINNIE.

And milk ?

HORACE.

[*After bowing assent.*]   We are a perfect Congress.

MINNIE.

[*To herself.*] I wonder what he wants with Clem.
[*To* HORACE.]   So glad you called to consult Mr.
Hale.

HORACE.

Consult ?

MINNIE.

[*Handing him a cup of tea.*] He's studying for
the bar, you know.   I thought perhaps —

HORACE.

Oh, yes, certainly.   I require his opinion on a
matter of extreme delicacy.

MINNIE.

[*Looking away chilled.*]   Oh !

HORACE.

[*Watching her over his cup.*] Congress has risen.
[*Leaning towards her.*]   Will you permit me to
acquaint you with my delicate business ?

MINNIE.

[*Very coldly.*]   Oh, really, Mr. Bream, I — I
think —

HORACE.

Miss Gilfillian, *you* are my delicate business.

MINNIE.

[*Rising quickly and haughtily.*] Indeed!

HORACE.

[*Contemplating her.*] Now, how thoroughly characteristic that is of this old country. [*Rising with his hat and cane.*] Miss Gilfillian. [*He goes to her — she moves away. He retreats, carefully choosing his position by selecting a particular spot in the pattern of the carpet with the end of his cane.*] Miss Gilfillian, the time I have spent in your society and in that of your delightful mother has been extremely fascinating to me

MINNIE.

[*Distantly.*] Oh, thank you. [*Advancing a step or two.*] I need not say I shall always remember gratefully the service you rendered me in Paris.

HORACE.

Pray don't allude to that. I — [*He goes towards her; she retreats to her former position. After a slight pause, he identifies his particular spot on the carpet and returns to it.*] But, Miss Gilfillian, I cert'nly did hope that those enchanting moments in Nice and in Monte Carlo, where I had the honour of instructing you in *Trente et Quarante*, might be continued in this — dear old country. And that's why I'm here to consult my friend Hale.

MINNIE.

[*Firing up.*] Pray, what has Mr. Hale to do with it?

HORACE.

Miss Gilfillian, you drove in the park yesterday
— with my friend Hale.

MINNIE.

Certainly.

HORACE.

I was there — hanging on to the railings. You
were at Cristofaro's concert in the evening — with
my friend Hale.

MINNIE.

[*Haughtily.*]   I was.

HORACE.

I was there — half over the balcony.

MINNIE.

Really — I —

HORACE.

This morning you were in and out all the stores
in Bond Street — I was balancing myself on the
curb. You had luncheon at a restaurant in Picca-
dilly, where they sell flies and other candies. It
was there I partook of a last season's ice.

MINNIE.

[*Losing her temper.*]   Oh!

HORACE.

I followed to every picture gallery within a mile
of the Burlington, in the dark rooms of which
I had a peaceful time. In fact, Miss Gilfillian, I
have the honour to be always with you.

MINNIE.

[*Angrily*]. I never see you, sir.

HORACE.

I trust I know better than to intrude.

MINNIE.

Where do you learn our movements ?

HORACE.

At the hotel.

MINNIE.

[*Indignantly*.] You present yourself at our hotel !

HORACE.

You are staying at my hotel.

MINNIE.

Oh ! On the same floor, I presume.

HORACE.

No.

MINNIE.

[*Sarcastically*.] Thank you.

HORACE.

I occupy the room immediately beneath your own.

MINNIE.

To listen to my movements !

HORACE.

To enjoy the consolation of conjecture.

MINNIE.

Oh! I can't tell you how indignant I am!

HORACE.

[*To himself.*] Well, I never thought a man could enjoy so much conversation with a young unmarried lady in this — old country.

MINNIE.

Oh! May I ask where you're going to-night?

HORACE.

I have a stall for the Cabinet Theatre.
> [*With a blank look* MINNIE *sinks upon the sofa.*

MINNIE.

I shall tell Mr. Hale.

HORACE.

Ah, if you will allow me, *I* will tell Mr. Hale. I'm here for that purpose. I'm here to ask my friend Hale whether he's fortunate enough to be engaged to the most fascinating lady I have ever known : and if he says Yes, I start for N'York on Saturday.

MINNIE.

[*Horrified.*] But if he says No!

HORACE.

Then I shall ask permission to rejoin your most delightful party.

MINNIE.

Oh!

CLEMENT *enters, dressed for the theatre.*

CLEMENT.

Half-past eight.

[MINNIE, *much disturbed, runs up to him.*

MINNIE.

Clement, here is that Mr. Bream.

CLEMENT.

Eh? [*Seeing* HORACE *and nodding distantly.*] How d'ye do?

[HORACE *returns* CLEMENT'S *salutation with a genial wave of the hand.*

HORACE.

How are you?

CLEMENT.

[*Softly to* MINNIE.] What's he doing here?

MINNIE.

[*To* CLEMENT.] Just what he does everywhere. He's the original little old man of the sea! [*Stamping her foot.*] He — he must be awfully fond of mamma!

CLEMENT.

[*To himself.*] We can't snub him after his splendid behaviour in Paris. Poor fellow! I wonder if he would join our theatre party. [*To* HORACE.] We're going to the Cabinet Theatre, Mr. Bream. I'm sure my aunt will be very pleased to see you in her box, if you —

MINNIE.

Oh!

CLEMENT.

It holds four.

HORACE.

[*Shaking hands with* CLEMENT.] Sir, it shall hold one who is eternally obliged to you.

MINNIE.

[*Distractedly.*] It's Fate!

Enter DICK, *in dilapidated evening dress, old opera hat and seedy gloves.*

CLEMENT.

[*Surprised.*] Why, Dick — I —

DICK.

Hadn't the heart to disoblige you, Clement, my boy.

CLEMENT.

I have just asked Mr. Bream to take the fourth seat in the box.

MINNIE.

I'm sure Mr. Bream will see that Mr. Phenyl has the first claim.

HORACE.

[*Bowing.*] Oh, cert'nly. [*To himself.*] That's just cruel, anyway.

DICK.

[*Clapping his hat on the mantelpiece and hastily removing his gloves.*] Couldn't think of it! Happy release for all parties.

HORACE.

[*Throwing his hat in the air and catching it.*] Ha!

MINNIE.

[*To herself.*] It *is* Fate!

> [*There is a very pronounced rat-tat-tat at the outer door.*

MINNIE.

My mamma!

HORACE.

[*To himself.*] And, I hope, mine.

CLEMENT.

[*To* DICK.] That's aunt, Dick.

DICK.

Auntie, undoubtedly.

CLEMENT.

[*Hesitatingly.*] Will you — er?

DICK.

No, Clement, my boy. I opened the door last — *your* turn.

[DICK *joins* HORACE *and* MINNIE. CLEM-
ENT *goes to the door and opens it.* MRS.
GILFILLIAN *is seen outside, dressed for
the theatre.*

MRS. GILFILLIAN.

Clement ! Is Minnie here ?

CLEMENT.

Yes, aunt. Won't you come in ?

MRS. GILFILLIAN.

Come in ? Of course I'll come in. [*Entering.*]
Minnie !

MINNIE.

Mamma !

MRS. GILFILLIAN.

[*Indignantly.*] Don't speak to me ! A young
girl ! You who taught in a Sunday-school at Barnchester. Don't speak to me ! What have you to
say for yourself ?

CLEMENT.

[*Arranging the armchair for her.*] My dear
aunt —

MRS. GILFILLIAN.

Go away, Clement. [*Breathlessly, sinking into the
armchair.*] How did you get here ?

MINNIE.

A hansom, mamma.

MRS. GILFILLIAN.

How dare you ! An unmarried girl in a hansom !

MINNIE.

They're quicker than four-wheelers, mamma.

MRS. GILFILLIAN.

Quicker! They're faster. I never drove in hansoms alone till I was thirty-three, and then I made the driver promise not to look at me through the roof.

MINNIE.

They never do that when you're alone. Mamma — [*coaxing*] — and, indeed, I'm very sorry.

MRS. GILFILLIAN.

Sorry!

MINNIE.

I wanted to speak to Clement — just by ourselves — there!

MRS. GILFILLIAN.

You haven't quarrelled!

MINNIE.

Quarrelled! No. We understand each other better now than we have ever done.

MRS. GILFILLIAN.

[*Patting* MINNIE's *cheek approvingly.*] Perhaps I've been a little too cross with you. [*In a whisper.*] But you must tell me everything to-night before you close your eyes. Mind — everything!

MINNIE.

Yes — everything!

Mrs. Gilfillian.

[*Triumphantly, to herself.*]   It's settled!   I'm sure of it!

Clement.

[*Looking at his watch.*]   Shall we start, aunt?

Mrs. Gilfillian.

[*Looking at him beamingly, and boxing his ears playfully with her fan.*]   The carriage is waiting. You bad boy!

[*Unnoticed,* Dick *stands looking on.*

Clement.

I hope you'll forgive me, aunt, for providing a fourth occupant to your box.

Mrs. Gilfillian.

Not that Mr. Funnel!

Dick.

No.

Mrs. Gilfillian.

[*Turning.*]   Oh!   [*To* Dick *apologetically.*]   I — really — I —

Clement.

Mr. Bream, aunt!

Mrs. Gilfillian.

[*Turning round and coming face to face with* Horace.]   Mr. Bream!

[HORACE *talks to* MRS. GILFILLIAN, DICK
chuckling at them.

MINNIE.

[*Quietly to* CLEMENT.] Clem, I must ask your
advice about Mr. Bream, directly.

CLEMENT.

Delighted. [*Assisting* MINNIE *to put on mantle.*]
Bream, will you drive on with my aunt to the
theatre ? Minnie and I want to walk up to Brigg's,
the florist's by Middle Temple Gate. We'll follow
you in a cab.

MRS. GILFILLIAN.

[*To herself.*] They *have* settled it ! [*Shaking her
fan at* CLEMENT.] Ah — h — h ! you sly boy. [*Good
humouredly taking* HORACE'S *arm.*] We're encum-
brances. Come along, Mr. Bream !

HORACE.

[*Ruefully to himself.*] Damn !
[*He takes* MRS. GILFILLIAN *out, leaving
the door open.*

CLEMENT.

Good-night, Dick. [*Warningly.*] Word of honour as usual !

DICK.

[*To* CLEMENT, *loftily.*] Word of honour, as usual,
Clement, my boy.

MINNIE.

Good-night, Mr. Phenyl. So sorry you are not coming with us. Is the florist's far?

DICK.

Two minutes.

CLEMENT.

We can make it ten by going round. It's a fine night.

> [*As* MINNIE *and* CLEMENT *go out*, BULGER *passes them and enters hastily.*

CLEMENT.

[*Outside.*] Ah! Mr. Bulger.

> [CLEMENT *closes the door.* DICK *turns and almost catches* BULGER *in his arms.* BULGER, *who is dressed in his best, is very agitated.*

BULGER.

Mr. Phenyl!

DICK.

What's the matter?

> [BULGER *drops faintly into the armchair, and wipes his brow with a coloured handkerchief.*

BULGER.

Excuse me for setting, sir; oh! Mr. Phenyl.

DICK.

I wish you wouldn't look as if you expected me to shave you, Bulger. You're not ill, I hope?

BULGER.

You and me has known Mrs. Rolt the same len'th o' time, Mr. Phenyl.

DICK.

What of her?

BULGER.

There's no need for secrecy no longer, sir. I 'ave regarded Mrs. Rolt very deeply for years, sir.

DICK.

Bulger!

BULGER.

Ridickleous it seems, most likely—I don't deny it.

DICK.

Of course it's ridiculous.

BULGER.

[*Angrily.*] I tell you I don't deny it, sir! But it's 'ard to keep our place iu this world when the place is a mean small one, and I 'ave so far forgot myself concerning Ruth Rolt as to drop into poetry.

[*He produces a folded paper from his hat.* DICK *shrinks away.*

DICK.

No!

BULGER.

Don't fear, sir. But this ev'ning while 'anging about the railin's downstairs — more like a thief than an old-established hairdresser — 'oping for a chance to slip this into Mrs. R.'s 'and, I — I saw what's brought me up to you, Mr. Phenyl.

DICK.

What have you seen, Bulger?

BULGER.

Peerin' over the top of the blind I see her little hornaments vanished from the mantelpiece, sir, and her few pictures took down — and — and —

DICK.

Bulger! what does it mean?

BULGER.

It honly means one thing to my mind. Ruth Rolt's a-goin', Mr. Phenyl.

DICK.

Going! Going away!

BULGER.

[*Pacing distractedly up and down the room.*] Goin', after all these years.

DICK.

Wait!

[DICK *runs excitedly up to the outer door, opens it and goes out. He returns directly, drawing the curtain over the passage opening.*

DICK.

[*Breathlessly, holding the curtain.*]   Bulger!

DICK.

[*Pointing to the door of his bedroom.*]　Get out of the way!　Wait in that room.

[BULGER *goes into* DICK'*s bedroom.　The curtain is then pushed aside and* RUTH, *in outgoing attire, looks in.*

RUTH.

Mr. Phenyl!

DICK.

[*With assumed lightness.*]　Ah, Ruth!

RUTH.

I've seen Mr. Hale go out with his friends; is there any chance of his returning till late?

DICK.

They're off to the play.　He won't be back till past eleven.　　　　　[*She drops the curtain.*

DICK.

What's this?　What's this?

RUTH.

[*Outside, calling softly.*]　Lavender!　Lavender!

DICK.

Lavender!　[RUTH *pushes aside the curtain and enters with* LAVENDER, *who is also dressed for going out, while her face is pale, her eyes red with weeping.*]　Why, Lavvy!

Ruth.

[*Pressing* Lavender *to her.*] Don't speak to her. She can't bear it.

Dick.

Ruth, what are you doing ?

Ruth.

Running away, people will call it; but we're out of debt, so that doesn't matter. We've come to say— good-bye, Mr. Phenyl.

Dick.

Good-bye, Ruth ! Not good-bye !

> [Lavender *gives a little cry of pain;* Ruth
> *places her in the armchair, then speaks
> to* Dick *apart.*

Ruth.

You've been a kind friend to us for fifteen years, Mr. Phenyl, but I'd have gone without troubling you, because you won't understand. But Lavvy begged so hard to look at this room once more, and I trust you not to hinder us ; I know I can trust you.

> [*She leaves him and leans her head on the
> back of the chair, weeping.*

Dick.

You're not going to hide yourselves away from Mr. Hale ?   [Lavender *starts up with a cry.*

Lavender.

Oh, yes, yes!

RUTH.

Mr. Hale! Why did he ever come here to bring this sorrow on me — to rob me of my little girl's love? What is Mr. Hale to me? I was rich before he came, because of her. My poor rooms were warm and well-furnished — all because of her. Yesterday any grand lady might have envied me — because of her. [*Indignantly.*] Mr. Hale, indeed!

LAVENDER.

Mother! I'm doing what you ask me, without complaining. But don't — don't speak against Mr. Hale any more.

DICK.

[*Fiercely.*] Speak against Mr. Hale! Who does? Ruth, who's at the bottom of this? I'll know — I'll know, before I let this boy's heart be broken as well as Lavvy's!

[LAVENDER *goes to* DICK *and lays her head upon his shoulder, sobbing.*

LAVENDER.

Oh, Mr. Phenyl! Will it break his heart? Will it — will it?

RUTH.

[*To* DICK, *despairingly.*] You'll undo all I've done. Don't! don't!

[DICK *puts* LAVENDER *from him gently. She goes and sits weeping on the window seat.*

DICK.

Now, look here, Ruth Rolt!

RUTH.

Hush! Mr. Phenyl, I'm deceiving her!

DICK.

Deceiving her?

RUTH.

I'm forcing her to do this! I've begged to her, gone down on my knees to her, made her promise not to forsake me. I've told her that if Mr. Hale married her, his rich friends would turn their backs on him, and that he'd soon weary of a wife who'd brought him only poverty. I've taught her that a true woman best proves her love for a man by thinking of his future. But, Heaven forgive me, that's not why I'm doing this — that's not why!

DICK.

Then there's no reason at all, Ruth, and you sha'n't do it! I say, you sha'n't do it!

RUTH.

Oh, pity me! I'll tell you! If Lavender ever married Mr. Hale she would have to be told the secret of my life.

DICK.

[*In a whisper.*] The secret, Ruth!

RUTH.

Yes. I pray for all women who hug such a secret to their bosom as I have always with me to keep me company. It would have worn me out years ago but for one blessing, one consolation — my child's respect for her mother. I've no right to it, but it has made my life endurable, even happy, and — imagine what it would be for me to lose it now !

> [DICK *holds out his hand; she turns and takes it.*

DICK.

[*Falteringly.*] Ruth, did I speak crossly to you? Ruth, did I? I — I'm sorry ; Lord forgive me — what a trouble and a worry I've been to you these fifteen years !

> [RUTH *leans upon the armchair, weeping.* LAVENDER *comes to* DICK.

LAVENDER.

[*Faintly.*] Mother, may I sit with Mr. Phenyl, if he'll let me, till it's time for us to start ?

DICK.

[*Patting her head.*] Of course, Lavvy — of course.

RUTH.

[*In a whisper to* DICK.] Oh, tell her that what I do is right. I know she'll never love me again as she has loved me ; but be my friend and defend me, Mr. Phenyl. [*To* LAVENDER, *as she is going towards the door.*] In ten minutes, Lavender.

LAVENDER.

Yes, mother.

DICK.

[*Following* RUTH.] You won't confide in me where you're going, Ruth ?

RUTH.

Don't ask me — even *she* doesn't know yet. Good-bye.

DICK.

[*Taking her hand.*] Ah, Ruth — fifteen years — fifteen years.

RUTH.

[*Tearfully.*] I remember many, many kindnesses to me and my little one. [*Raising his hand to her lips.*] Good-bye, Mr. Phenyl. [*She goes out.*

DICK.

[*To himself, as he goes to the armchair and sinks into it.*] Good-bye, Ruth, good-bye. Fifteen years! Fifteen years!

LAVENDER.

Mr. Phenyl!

DICK.

Lavender!

LAVENDER.

Is it true, Mr. Phenyl?

DICK.

Is what true?

LAVENDER.

Mother says that Mr. Hale's friends would turn against him if he married me ; would they ? She says that he'd dote on me for a time, and treat me like a child does a doll, and then he'd grow tired of me and fret for what he'd lost by choosing a toy-wife instead of a lady. Is that true, Mr. Phenyl?

DICK.

[*Distressed.*]   Lavvy, you do ask such questions !

LAVENDER.

You know him very well ; perhaps he's talked to you a little about me.   I'll believe you if you tell me I'm not fit for him.   Is it true, Mr. Phenyl, is it true ?

> [*She breaks down, and sinking on her knees, bows her head on the arm of the chair, and sobs.*

DICK.

[*Hesitatingly.*]   Lavvy — I —

LAVENDER.

[*Crying.*]   Oh, it's not true, is it ?

DICK.

[*With an effort.*]   Yes, Lavvy, it's true.

LAVENDER.

[*Faintly.*]   Oh !

DICK.

It's the way of the world for poverty to make us sour and unjust ; and if Clem came to grief he might lay it at the door of the little doll's house which contained the little doll he'd married.

LAVENDER.

[*Rising, and drawing back.*]   Oh, I don't believe that of Clem.

DICK.

[*Starting up and following her.*] No — nor I!

LAVENDER.

Ah!

DICK.

[*Checking himself.*] But — your mother knows better than we do! — your mother knows better than we do! So you must go downstairs now, Lavvy. It's quite time you went downstairs to your mother.

LAVENDER.

I wanted you to let me write a letter here, just saying good-bye to Clement; but now you send me downstairs.

DICK.

[*Not looking at her.*] Be quick, then, be quick.

LAVENDER.

Yes, I'll be quick.

     [*She goes to the writing-table, and sits writing.*

DICK.

[*Eyeing* LAVENDER, *guiltily.*] I'm behaving remarkably well to Clement, I am. I'm a valuable friend for a young gentleman to board with and confide in, I flatter myself! Ugh!

LAVENDER.

[*Writing.*] "My dear — my dear —" [*To herself.*] How can I call him my dear; he's not *my* dear!

[*She sobs.* DICK *hears her and starts, put-*
ting his fingers in his ears.

DICK.

[*Helplessly.*] Why did I promise to help Ruth ?

LAVENDER.

Oh, Clement, Clement !

DICK.

[*To himself.*] Poor Clem ! I shall never be able
to look him in the face again. I — I —

[*He works his mouth as if his tongue were dry,*
then desperately looks into the teapot.

LAVENDER.

[*Writing.*] "It's for your good — I'm going
away." [*With another sob.*] Ah !

DICK.

[*Shutting the lid of the teapot.*] Empty.

[*He starts up, looks round quickly, then goes*
to the sideboard, stooping down and open-
ing the cupboard, while he glances over
his shoulder at LAVENDER.

LAVENDER.

[*Resting her head upon the table.*] Oh, I can't.
I can't.

[DICK *takes a decanter of whiskey and the*
carafe and tumbler from the sideboard
and brings them to the table.

DICK.

[*To himself.*] The last time, Clement, my boy
—the last time. [*He pours some whiskey into the
tumbler and gulps it. It makes him cough: he looks
round at* LAVENDER *guiltily, then draws the left side
of the large curtain over the opening to the further
room.*] Only a thimbleful, Clement, my boy.
[*Pouring out more whiskey and drinking it; then
sitting and staring at the tumbler.*] I — I've broken
my word to Clement. [*Drinking.*] If Clem were
to come back now by chance he'd see me —. [*Suddenly.*] He'd see *her* —. Oh! [*He drains his
glass and rises excitedly.*] Clemen', my boy! Why
shouldn't you come back now — by chance? [*He
goes to the table and scribbles a few words on a piece
of paper, which he hastily encloses in an envelope.*]
Bulger! Where did I put Bulger? [*Recollecting.*]
Bulger! [*Going hastily to the door of his bedroom,
opening it, and calling in a whisper.*] Bulger!
[BULGER *appears in the doorway.* DICK *seizes him
and gives him the note.*] Run up to Brigg's, the
florist. If you catch Mr. Hale there, give him that.
Run, Bulger, run — run! [*He hurries* BULGER *out.*]
Now, I've broken my word to poor Ruth. [*Weakly.*]
Bulger! [*Going to the door again, opening it, and
calling faintly.*] Bulger? Don't run — walk!

MR. MAW, *a white-haired old gentleman in an In-
verness cape, with a crisp, dry manner of speak-
ing, appears outside.*

MAW.

Oh, I'm lucky, Mr. Phenyl. May I speak to
you on a matter of great importance?

DICK.

[*Closing the door.*]   Mr. Maw, I think ?]

MAW.

Yes.   I am very late in leaving my office to-night, and seeing your light in your window —.   [*Staring at* DICK.]   I hope you're well ?

DICK.

[*Drawing himself up with dignity.*]   Qui' well, than'g you.   Take a chair.

MAW.

[*Sitting — to himself.*]   This man is in his usual condition, I'm afraid.

DICK.

[*Drawing the right side of the large curtain to meet the left side, completely hiding the further room from view.*]   Excuse me, Lavvy — two minutes — two minutes.

> [*He walks with rather uncertain steps to a chair and sits, mixing some whiskey and water.*

MAW.

[*Taking some papers from his pocket — eyeing* DICK.]   Well, well, perhaps it's better !   I really pity him.

DICK.

[*Drinking.*]   Broken my word to Ruth.

MAW.

[*Selecting from his papers a letter with a deep mourning border.*]   Mr. Phenyl.

DICK.

[*With a wave of the hand towards the decanter.*] Join me ?

MAW.

[*Sharply.*] No, thank you.

DICK.

No. [*Getting quite muddled.*] If you don't take weak drop whiskey an' wa'er after the labours of the day, when *do* you take weak drop whiskey an' wa'er ?

MAW.

Never, sir. Mr. Phenyl, your late mother's brother, Mr. Vipont —

DICK.

Uncle George. [*Snapping his fingers indignantly.*] I washed my han's of him twen'y years ago — on account of his habits. I should say *my* habits.

[*Drinking again.*

MAW.

If you'd kindly postpone your — supper till I've gone I should feel obliged. Mr. Phenyl, you will regret to hear that Mr. Vipont is dead.

[DICK *has his glass to his lips — he replaces it upon the table.*

DICK.

[*Whimpering.*] Poor Uncle George! A violent-tempered man, Mr. Maw — all blame, blame; but praise, oh dear, no! [*With a hiccough.*] Much might have been done by kindness.

MAW.

[*Shortly.*] Whatever lack of toleration your uncle displayed towards you, Mr. Phenyl, he neglected to destroy a will made years ago entirely in your favour.

DICK.

[*Rising unsteadily.*] My fav'ah! Will in — my fav'ah! My!

MAW.

[*Raising his hand.*] But, Mr. Phenyl —

DICK.

[*Swaying to and fro over* MAW.] But! Oh, I p'ceive. My poor uncle resembled his poor nephew — never thought of the rainy day when he'd want a pound or two to die with.

MAW.

I beg your pardon. I have a schedule here of bonds and other easily negotiable securities, deposited with his bankers, of the value of twenty-five thousand pounds.

DICK.

[*With his hand to his head.*] Wai'! Wai'! Twen'y-five thousan'—

MAW.

Beyond that I trace a further fifteen thousand entrusted to these bankers for investment at their discretion.

[DICK *falls into his chair and gulps at his drink.*

DICK.

[*Incoherently.*] Twen'y-five thousan' — fifteen thousan' — for'y thousan" —

MAW.

But, Mr. Phenyl, I've not yet told you everything.

DICK.

[*Waving him away.*] For'y thousan' — that's sufficient !

MAW.

I've told you that Mr. Vipont's fortune was in the hands of his *bankers*.

DICK.

[*Drinking.*] Long life to the bankers !

MAW.

It is the old tale, sir — over-speculation, temptation, false balance sheets. To-day the doors of the bank to which Mr. Vipont entrusted his fortune have been finally closed.

DICK.

Broke !

MAW.

[*Producing a telegram.*] This telegram informs me that two of the partners have absconded. It's a bad business, Mr. Phenyl.

DICK.

[*Blankly.*] Flight of — for'y — thousan' partners ! [*Taking the telegram from* MAW *and looking at it stupidly.*] Uncle George's fortune.

[*Rustling the telegram and looking through it as if it were a bank-note.*] Largest bank-note I've ever had in my life.

> [*Sticking the telegram in his waistcoat pocket,* DICK *staggers across the room as the door opens and* CLEMENT *enters with* DICK'S *note in his hand.*

CLEMENT.

[*Breathlessly.*] Dick!

DICK.

Clemen', my boy!

> [CLEMENT *comes upon* DICK *who is sitting helplessly on the arm of the chair.*

CLEMENT.

[*Starting back.*] Dick! You've been — drinking!

DICK.

No. [*Pointing to* MAW.] My s'litor, Mr. Maw.

MAW.

[*Brusquely.*] Mr. Phenyl isn't very well, I'm afraid.

DICK.

[*To* MAW.] The spirits are with you, Mr. Maw.

MAW.

I'll see Mr. Phenyl in the morning.

> [MAW *goes out and shuts door.*

CLEMENT.

[*Pulling* DICK *up.*]   Dick, speak to me! What's the meaning of this note?

DICK.

Ban'g note, Clemen'.   For'y thousan' pounds.

CLEMENT.

[*Shaking* DICK'S *arm.*]   Dick! there's no bad news of Lavender.

DICK.

[*Slightly reviving.*]   Lavender! Oh — I remember. [*Pointing toward the curtains.*]   Impor'ant letter from Lavender in the nex' room.

CLEMENT.

A letter!   Thank you for sending after me, but I wouldn't have come back to see you like this, not even for a letter from Lavender.   Dick, I'll never trust you again!

> [*He goes through the curtains, closing them after him.*

DICK.

[*Piteously.*]   Oh, do forgive me, Clemen'! do overlook it!

> [*There is the sound of a cry from* LAVENDER.

LAVENDER.

[*On the other side of the curtains.*]   Ah, Clement!

DICK.

[*Listening.*]   Ah! you'll forgive me now, Clem-

en', won't you ? It's Ruth who'll never forgive me.
I'll hide from Ruth ! I can't face Ruth ! [*Taking up the decanter and tumbler and crossing to the
door of his bedroom.*] The las' time, Clemen', my
boy — the las' time !

> [*He stumbles out, as* CLEMENT *comes through
> the curtains supporting* LAVENDER. *He
> places her gently upon the sofa.*

CLEMENT.

[*In a whisper.*] Dick — I didn't mean what I
said. I —

LAVENDER.

[*Opening her eyes.*] Clement !

CLEMENT.

[*Bending over her.*] Lavender !

LAVENDER.

The letter — the letter I was writing to you !
Fetch it.

CLEMENT.

The letter !

> [*He disappears through the curtain.*

LAVENDER.

He mustn't find out to-night that mother is taking
me away !

> [CLEMENT *re-enters with the letter.*

CLEMENT.

Won't you give it to me ?

LAVENDER.

By-and-bye! by-and-bye!

[*He gives her the letter — she thrusts it into her pocket with a sigh of relief.*

CLEMENT.

My poor little sweetheart, are these the red cheeks you promised? Is this how you keep faith with me?

LAVENDER.

I meant to keep faith with you always, Clement.

[*Covering her face with her hands.*

CLEMENT.

Ah, I'm not scolding you. How brave of you to struggle up all these stairs to ease my suspense. But won't you say that you're better — a little better — for seeing me?

LAVENDER.

[*Falteringly.*] Yes; I — I — But you startled me so, Clement!

CLEMENT.

[*Putting his arm round her.*] Why, what a delicate little flower it is, and how I shall have to tend it and nurture it all my life!

LAVENDER.

All — your — life! All your life!

[*She takes his hand from her shoulder and throws it almost roughly from her — then rises in agitation.*

CLEMENT.

[Startled.] Lavender!

LAVENDER.

[*Under her breath, clasping her hands.*] Mother! don't take me away! Don't, don't take me away!

CLEMENT.

Lavender! You're angry with me.

LAVENDER.

[*Pointing to the clock.*] No; but I'd forgotten — Mother is waiting for me. Good-night, Clement.

CLEMENT.

Ah, no — not yet.

LAVENDER.

I must — I — I promised. And, Clement, you *have* been very troubled about me, the few hours we've been separated, haven't you?

CLEMENT.

Troubled! If you only knew!

LAVENDER.

Well, then, dear, I want you to remember, if ever we're parted again —

CLEMENT.

No — not again, Lavender.

LAVENDER.

I mean, if ever you have to go upon a journey, or I —have — to go —a journey — I want you to bear in mind that my thoughts are true and faithful and loving to you.

CLEMENT.

My sweet Lavender!

LAVENDER.

And though I'm a poor commonplace girl, and you're far above me, my prayers for you are just as good as any lady's, and they shall never cease, night or morning — never, dear, never, not as long as I live. [*Taking the letter from her pocket, and giving it to him timidly.*] There's the letter I wrote to you. You must give me your word you'll not open it till the morning.

CLEMENT.

I do give you my word.

LAVENDER.

Let me see you hide it away somewhere: in the next room, or —

CLEMENT.

[*With a smile.*] Certainly. I'll lock it up there. [*Going to the writing-table, and unlocking the drawer, he puts the letter away, talking, while his back is turned towards* LAVENDER.] There! When I open this drawer to-morrow these old bills will have doubled themselves with pride. What have they done to deserve such sweet company?

[*Seizing her opportunity, with a last look
at* CLEMENT, *she goes softly up to the
outer door. As she reaches it there is a
loud rat-tat-tat, and, with a cry, she
comes back into the room.*

LAVENDER.

Clement!

CLEMENT.

[*Turning.*]   Hullo!   A caller for Dick, I expect.
Whoever it is, he doesn't come in.

[*He goes up to the outer door and opens it.*
MR. GEOFFREY WEDDERBURN *is outside.*

WEDDERBURN.

[*Heartily.*]   Clement, my dear lad!

CLEMENT.

Father!

[*With a low cry,* LAVENDER *disappears
through the curtain, as* WEDDERBURN
enters, while CLEMENT, *having closed the
door, looks around for her.* GEOFFREY
WEDDERBURN *is a handsome, well-pre-
served man of about fifty with a ruddy
face, a bright cheery voice with a slight
burr in it, and the air and manner of a
prosperous country gentleman. He is
dressed in tweeds and an ulster, as if
from a journey. He throws his hat and
gloves upon the sofa, then turns to*
CLEMENT *with open arms.*

WEDDERBURN.

Come here! [*Affectionately.*] Lord, how glad I am to see you!

CLEMENT.

[*Taking his hand.*] Ah, father, now that I hear your kind voice I feel how neglectful I've been. You look well.

WEDDERBURN.

Look well! Ha, ha! [*Playfully.*] I haven't a little love affair on hand, you villain!

[*Throwing his ulster upon the sofa.*

CLEMENT.

Dad, you know!

WEDDERBURN.

Know! All the world knows when a terrible chap like you is in love.

CLEMENT.

[*Embarrassed.*] I was going to write to you to-night.

WEDDERBURN.

Don't you trouble yourself, Clem. [*Taking a bundle of letters and papers from his pocket.*] Your Aunt Clara's telegram gives a few interesting particulars.

CLEMENT.

Mrs. Gilfillian's telegram!

WEDDERBURN.

Why, what dy'e think has brought me from Paris in such a deuce of a hurry — eh?

CLEMENT.

And you're not angry, father ?

WEDDERBURN.

Angry.   Now, have I ever been angry with you,
my boy ?

CLEMENT.

No, dad — never.

WEDDERBURN.

No, and a plague of a child you've been, too.

CLEMENT.

[*Laughing.*]   Ha, ha !

WEDDERBURN.

[*Taking* CLEMENT'S *hand and looking into his
face.*]   But the only time you really hurt me, Clem,
was when you had the fever years ago, and I sat by
your bedside through some dreadful nights and —
you didn't know me when I spoke to you.   Ah,
Clem !

CLEMENT.

[*Putting his hand on* WEDDERBURN'S *shoulder.*]
Ah, dad !

WEDDERBURN.

However, confound that !   [*Selecting a telegram
from among his letters and looking at it through a
gold-rimmed eye-glass.*]   And so she's the daughter
of the laundress of these new chambers of yours, is
she, Clement ?

CLEMENT.

[*Biting his lip.*]   Yes, father, but —

WEDDERBURN.

But she's very beautiful, hey ?

CLEMENT.

She's very sweet, very good —

WEDDERBURN.

[*Reading the telegram.*]   Oh, I know, my dear lad — I know.

CLEMENT.

Father, would you like to see her — this evening ?

[WEDDERBURN *returns his papers to his pocket and rises, putting his arm round* CLEMENT'S *shoulder.*

WEDDERBURN.

Now, my dear Clement, why on earth should I see her ?

CLEMENT.

[*Under his breath.*]   Father!

WEDDERBURN.

Come, come, we'll have a bit of a jaunt together, you and I.   They don't want me at the bank — I'm only a name there nowadays; but for form's sake we'll run down to Barnchester in the morning, and then we'll cut away North and be lazy and happy. Look sharp; tell your man to throw a few things into a portmanteau, and come back with me to the hotel to-night.   [*Taking up his hat and coat.*

CLEMENT.

Dad ! You — you don't understand. I can
never leave here until — Father, Lavender is to be
my wife !

[WEDDERBURN *stands for a moment thought-*
fully, then throws down his hat and coat
and crosses to the fireplace, taking a
cigar from his cigar-case, while CLEMENT
watches him.

WEDDERBURN.

Clement, my dear boy, my son, when I was a
young man — old enough to know better, but
a young man — I fell in love with a woman just as
enchanting, I dare swear, as this Miss — Lavender,
as you call her.

CLEMENT.

Well, father ?

WEDDERBURN.

She was a woman in humble life but I loved her
— dearly. But just as I was on the point of marry-
ing her, Clem, my hard, old-fashioned common-
sense pulled me back.

CLEMENT.

Ah, sir ! — why ?

WEDDERBURN.

Why ? Why, my lady would have been all
elbows, as we say, among the starched gentlefolks
of Barnchester. She would have been mercilessly
cut by the whole county, Clement.

CLEMENT.

Then confound the whole county, sir.

WEDDERBURN.

Oh, by all means. But the neglect would have
soured her and made me cross, and it would have
been a damned wretched marriage. That's all, my
boy. [*Taking* CLEMENT's *hand.*] But, Clem, it
nearly broke me up at that time, and to find some
corner to hide my love in, I made a son of the child
of a dear dead schoolfellow of mine.

CLEMENT.

Sir, I can't ever repay you.

WEDDERBURN.

Yes, you can — all the payment I want you can
make me to-night. What I did for common-sense
years ago you must do for me at this moment. So
put on your hat and come along.

[*Goes to sofa and takes up coat and hat.*

CLEMENT.

I — I can't, father.

WEDDERBURN.

[*Sharply.*] You — you won't, you mean?

CLEMENT.

Father!

WEDDERBURN.

She or I — which is it?

CLEMENT.

God bless you for all your goodness to me, sir; but she is to be my wife.

DICK.

[*Calling from his room.*] Clemen', my boy! Clemen'!

WEDDERBURN.

What's that?

CLEMENT.

[*Going towards the door of* DICK'S *room.*] Hush, Dick!

    [*The door opens, and* DICK *staggers on, flourishing the telegram which* MAW *has given him.*   `

DICK.

Clemen'! Look here! This telegram to my s'licitor! Look!

CLEMENT.

[*Trying to silence him.*] Be quiet, Dick! Mr. Wedderburn!

DICK.

Wedderburn!

WEDDERBURN.

May I ask the name of your friend?

CLEMENT.

Richard Phenyl. We share these rooms together.

WEDDERBURN.

[*Angrily, to* DICK.] Then, sir, I congratulate you on acquiring the undivided companionship of

Mr. Clement Hale, who can now accompany you to the gutter with all possible speed.

DICK.

[*Indignantly.*] The gurr'er!

WEDDERBURN.

The gutter, sir — which I take to be your destination.

DICK.

The gurr'er! [*Handing him the telegram.*] Then we can give you a lift, Mr. Wedderburn.

CLEMENT.

Dick, be silent!

WEDDERBURN.

What's this mean? [*Taking the telegram.*

DICK.

It means that Wedderburn, Green, and Hoskett, bankers, of Barnchester, have s'spended paymen'! Broke, sir, to atoms!

> [*There is a knocking at the outer door.* DICK *staggers up to it.* CLEMENT *goes to* WEDDERBURN, *who stands gazing steadily at the telegram.*

CLEMENT.

Father! You know better than to believe this. [*The knock is repeated.* WEDDERBURN *is silent.*] Father!

[DICK *opens the door and admits* MRS. GIL-
FILLIAN, MINNIE, *and* HORACE. *The two
former, seeing* WEDDERBURN, *go to him,
while* HORACE *speaks rapidly to* CLEMENT.
DICK, *leaving the door open, joins them.*

MRS. GILFILLIAN.

Geoffrey!

MINNIE.

Uncle! Uncle! [*Putting her arm round his
neck.*] There's some dreadful news in the paper —
about the bank, Uncle Geoffrey.

WEDDERBURN.

The paper — send for it; let me see it.

MRS. GILFILLIAN.

Geoffrey, it isn't true.

WEDDERBURN.

[*With an effort.*] Show me — the paper. [*Hear-
ing a movement, he turns sharply and sees* CLEMENT
reading from a newspaper which HORACE *holds.*]
You have it there — give it me. MRS. GILFILLIAN
sits weeping on the sofa; MINNIE *stands bending
over her consolingly.* CLEMENT *gives* WEDDERBURN
*the newspaper. After looking at the paper for a
moment,* WEDDERBURN, *with a groan, bows his head
upon the mantelpiece. In a smothered voice.*] The
villains! Dishonour! Dishonour!

RUTH.

[*Calling softly outside.*] Lavender! [*She enters
hurriedly.*] Lavender! [*To* CLEMENT, *seeing all*

but WEDDERBURN.]   Where is she ?   I want — my daughter.

> [CLEMENT *disappears through the curtains.* WEDDERBURN, *hearing* RUTH'S *voice, turns, and he and* RUTH *come face to face.*

WEDDERBURN.

[*In a whisper.*]   Ruth !

> [*They stand staring at each other.* LAVENDER *comes through the curtains. With an effort* RUTH *seizes her and goes out with her quickly. As they disappear* WEDDERBURN *puts his hand to his eyes and staggers, and* CLEMENT. *re-entering at that moment, catches him as he drops into the armchair fainting.*

CLEMENT.

Father !   Father !

END OF THE SECOND ACT.

The scene is the same as before, but the time is a week later.

CLEMENT, *looking weary and downhearted, comes from his bedroom.*

CLEMENT.

[*As he closes the door.*] Father, I shall be with you in half-an-hour.

> [*He takes up his hat, as* DICK, *improved in appearance, but without his coat, and wearing a housemaid's apron, and carrying a long carpet-broom, a dustpan, and a hand-broom, enters the room from the passage.*

DICK.

Going out, Clement, my boy?

CLEMENT.

Why, what are you doing, Dick?

DICK.

I've had a fierce, a terrible, altercation with Mrs.

McOstrich, the new woman downstairs; really a disgraceful row — on her part especially. She said if I hadn't been a man, she'd have struck me. Oh, what a change!

CLEMENT.

[*Despondently.*] Change! The house seems a hundred years older, now Lavender has gone.

DICK.

Yes, and a thousand years dirtier, now Ruth is gone. [*Cheerfully.*] However, poor Mrs. Gilfillian and Minnie sha'n't be put about, and so I rise to the occasion. [*Placing the dustpan and hand-broom on the sofa, and proceeding to turn up his shirt-sleeves.*] I've an excellent notion of thorough housework, Clement, my boy.

CLEMENT.

Dick, I'm ashamed of myself when I think what a splendid chap you've been all through this dreadful week.

DICK.

[*Good-humouredly.*] Pooh! Don't talk to me, sir! I certainly did prepare Mrs. Gilfillian's and Minnie's breakfast this morning; I don't deny that.

CLEMENT.

You!

DICK.

My dear Clem, a man who is on familiar terms with every grill in Fleet Street ought to know something about cooking. [*Resting his broom against the armchair, he takes up a covered dish from the*

table.] I don't wish to put side on over a few pal-
try foolish kidneys, but — [*raising the dish-cover*]
— confound it, they haven't looked at 'em.

CLEMENT.

[*Inspecting the dish with* DICK.] I'm afraid they
have, Dick.

DICK.

[*Indignantly.*] Of course! Go on! Blame,
blame — but praise, oh, dear, no! [*He takes up
the teapot, and begins to sprinkle the tea-leaves on
the floor angrily.*] If you're going out, I'll not
detain you. I am nervous when watched.

CLEMENT.

[*Not heeding him.*] I have to meet Mr. Maw at
half-past ten to hear the result of the meeting of
the bank creditors at Barnchester yesterday.

DICK.

Oh!

CLEMENT.

But the ship's hopelessly aground, Dick, and we
shall never get her off again — another bump or two
and she breaks up; a few spars float out seaward in
the shape of poor ruined depositors, and there's an
end. And what an end! Driven on to the rocks
by a couple of rogues while the skipper is asleep
below. There's a moral in it all, Dick.

DICK.

[*Sprinkling the tea-leaves.*] There is, Clement,

my boy. The moral will possibly assume the curt
and abbreviated form of sixpence in the pound.

CLEMENT.

Ah, you're thinking of old Mr. Vipont's fortune,
Dick — *your* fortune.

DICK.

No, I'm not! Don't be so unjust, Clem.

CLEMENT.

You'd have been a rich man.

DICK.

Clement, my boy, it would have been the ruin of
me! There is an appropriateness about a poor
vagabond, but a wealthy vagabond is an outrage
to society.

CLEMENT.

Society makes forty thousand excuses for forty
thousand pounds — while it lasts.

DICK.

It wouldn't have lasted. It might have induced
me to keep a cellar. Don't be sorry for me, Clem!
Be sorry for yourself, and for your people, but not
for a chap like me!

CLEMENT.

[*Wringing* DICK's *hand.*] Bless you, Dick! [DICK
continues sprinkling the tea-leaves.] I'll hurry back
with the result of yesterday's meeting, good or bad.

[CLEMENT *goes to the outer door where he
pauses.*

DICK.

[*Exultingly.*] I think the news will be a little better than you expect, Clement, my boy! [*Singing, with a few steps of a dance.*] La-d-diddle! La-d-diddle! La-di-diddle-da!

CLEMENT.

[*Returning.*] Oh, Dick!

[DICK *checks himself suddenly, and comes down, letting the tea run out of the spout of the teapot.*

DICK.

[*Enquiringly.*] Clement, my boy? Oh!

[*Replacing the teapot on the table and taking up the broom.*

CLEMENT.

[*Taking a slip of paper from his waistcoat pocket.*] I think you ought to know that I'm going to leave this at the newspaper office for insertion in tomorrow's paper. [*Reading.*] "Sweet Lavender." [*Showing him the paper.*] See, Dick? The first and last letters — all the rest stars.

DICK.

Very ingenious.

CLEMENT.

[*Reading.*] " R. P." (I've ventured to use your initials, old fellow.) " R. P. entreats his old friend and her daughter to communicate with him without delay. R. P. is distracted at their absence."

DICK.

[*Dubiously taking up the long broom.*] R. P.

CLEMENT.

I make you figure in it, Dick, to avoid distressing Mr. Wedderburn while he's ill. You see, nobody can possibly object to *your* being distracted.

DICK.

No, no — certainly not.

CLEMENT.

Whereas my poor Lavvy will understand, if ever she sees this, that it's I who am suffering. You don't mind, Dick ?

DICK.

My boy, delighted.

CLEMENT.

[*Producing* LAVENDER's *letter.*] I read her letter every hour of the day. To think that she imagined my love burnt so feebly that time or trouble could blow it out!

DICK.

[*Sweeping uncomfortably.*] Ah'm!

CLEMENT.

[*Indignantly.*] But it's so unlike her, Dick. I feel sure the confounded worldly philosophy was crammed into her dear little head by others.

DICK.

[*Sweeping wildly.*] Oh!

CLEMENT.

My aunt declares it is all Mrs. Rolt's doing. [*Returning the letter to his pocket fiercely.*] I hope so, for if I ever find out to the contrary — [DICK *sweeps up against* CLEMENT *violently.*] Confound you, Dick! What are you doing?

DICK.

You're hindering me! You're delaying the house-work! Go out!

CLEMENT.

Don't be angry with me. I'm going.

[CLEMENT *goes out.*

DICK.

[*Wiping his forehead.*] Phew! When he breaks out like that, I — I always break out like this. If he only suspected that I assisted at the cramming of the philosophy!

[MR. BULGER *comes from* CLEMENT'S *room carrying shaving paraphernalia.*

BULGER.

[*Very dejectedly.*] Good-morning, Mr. Phenyl. I rather fancy as Mr. Wedderburn is a trifle better this morning. He demanded to be shaved *up*, sir — always a sign of vitality in a gentleman.

[*He goes to the door of* DICK'S *bedroom, and has his hand on the handle, when* DICK *starts up with a cry of horror.*

DICK.

Where are you going?   Come back!

BULGER.

Good gracious, sir!   I understood I was to go
once over Mr. 'Ale's chin.   I perrysoom he is shar-
ing your room?

DICK.

Oh, lor', Bulger!   While Mr. Wedderburn is here,
nursed by his relatives, Mr. Hale and I billet ourselves at Chorley's Hotel, in Surrey Street.   We've
handed that room over to Mrs. Gilfillian and her
daughter.   You *should* be more careful, Bulger.

BULGER.

I'm extremely sorry; though, at the worst, I
daresay as an old family man, I could have passed
it off with a pleasantry.

[*There is a rat-tat at the outer door.*

DICK.

The doctor, *I* know.

BULGER.

I'll go, sir.   No noos of Mrs. Rolt, Mr. Phenyl?

DICK.

[*Taking off his apron and putting on his coat.*]
No, Bulger.

BULGER.

[*Sighing.*]   Ah!

[BULGER *opens the door and admits* DR.
DELANEY, *then goes out.*

DR. DELANEY.

[*As he enters.*] Thank ye, thank ye. [*Shaking hands with* DICK.] It's Mr. Phenyl. And how's our friend Wedderburn this delightful morning?

DICK.

Um — pretty well for a man who appears to grow a year older every day.

DR. DELANEY.

You don't say that?

DICK.

I do. It seems to me, Doctor Delaney, that your patient is aging on the tobogganing principle.

DR. DELANEY.

[*Thoughtfully.*] Ah — um!

DICK.

[*Enthusiastically.*] But the ladies, doctor! They come out gloriously.

DR. DELANEY.

Bless 'em, they always do.

DICK.

I wouldn't have believed it of aunt — Mrs. Gil-fillian. But she seems to have bought the good-will and fixtures of the business formerly carried on by Miss Nightingale.

DR. DELANEY.

My dear Mr. Phenyl, all ladies are aloike when

trouble takes their hair a little out of curl. It's
vanity and self-consciousness that spoil a woman,
sir; but when once she says to herself, "I don't
care a pin how I look," Heaven takes care that she
shall look like an angel. , However, that's no business of moine. I'll see Wedderburn.

DICK.

Oh, Doctor Delaney!

DR. DELANEY.

What is it?

DICK.

Do you observe any marked improvement in *me?*

DR. DELANEY.

Ah, I'm forgettin' you entirely. [*Feeling* DICK's
pulse.] What news?

DICK.

[*In a whisper.*] Not a drop for seven days.
That's a fearful drought, eh? I hesitate even at
gravy.

DR. DELANEY.

And how do you feel?

DICK.

A little weak, doctor — a little diluted. But I'm
firm.

DR. DELANEY.

Ah, you'll do very well. Mind, now, don't think
about it — and take plenty of exercise.

[DELANEY *raps at the door leading to* CLEM-
ENT'S *room then opens it, and goes out.*

DICK.

Exercise ! [*Removing his coat, then seizing his
broom and sweeping violently.*] Exercise ! [*Wiping his brow again.*] Phew ! This is rather dry
and dusty for my complaint. [*Sweeping.*] But
it's exercise.

[MINNIE, *dressed and simply wearing a pretty
white apron, comes from* DICK'S *room.*

MINNIE.

Oh, Mr. Phenyl, what are you doing ?

DICK.

[*Panting.*] Making up Doctor Delaney's pre-
scription. Please return to your room for a quarter
of an hour, Miss Gilfillian.

MINNIE.

[*Retreating.*] Oh, the dust ! [*Taking up the
hand-broom and dustpan from the sofa.*] And look
here !

[DICK *sweeps again.* MRS. GILFILLIAN,
*plainly dressed and without her curls,
comes from* CLEMENT'S *room.*

MRS. GILFILLIAN.

Mercy on us ! What's this ?

[*She throws open the window.*

MINNIE.

[*Laughing.*] Mr. Phenyl is sweeping, mamma.

MRS. GILFILLIAN.

Sweeping!   Where's that woman McOstrich?

DICK.

I regret to say that Mrs. McOstrich is in a condition of matutinal inebriation.

MRS. GILFILLIAN.

Ugh, how horrible!

MINNIE.

Oh, ma, how shocking!

DICK.

Ah! ladies, it is far more shocking to one who may claim some affinity with the misguided person now occupying the basement.

MRS. GILFILLIAN.

Ah'm!

MINNIE.

[*Kindly.*]   Oh, Mr. Phenyl!   [*To herself.*]   Poor man!

MRS. GILFILLIAN.

But this isn't sweeping, Mr. Phenyl — this is stirring up.

DICK.

[*Penitently.*]   No, Mrs. Gilfillian, it *is* sweeping. It is a shame-faced effort to sweep away a peculiarly useless and discreditable career.   It is also an attempt to throw dust in the eyes of two good-natured ladies — that being the only method by which I can hope to obtain their good opinion.

MRS. GILFILLIAN.

Bless the man! Take his broom away, Minnie — take his broom away!

[MINNIE *takes the broom from* DICK *and goes out with it.*

MRS. GILFILLIAN.

I wonder if I can guess what you allude to, Mr. Phenyl.

DICK.

[*Resuming his coat.*] Ah'm! I'll allow you three guesses, ma'am.

MRS. GILFILLIAN.

On the night we heard of our misfortune we saw you rather — at a disadvantage.

DICK.

Done, first time. I suppose I presented a shocking spectacle.

MRS. GILFILLIAN.

H'm! Well, that's a week ago, Mr. Phenyl. Now, Rome wasn't built in a day, but you can make a new man out of unpromising material in a week — and a new woman too — sometimes. Mr. Phenyl, I'm not the woman I was a week ago — am I?

DICK.

[*Hesitating.*] Well —

MRS. GILFILLIAN.

[*Sharply.*] Am I, sir?

DICK.

No.

MRS. GILFILLIAN.

I'm sure I'm not.   Now I've lost all my money
by the failure of the Barnchester Bank, but somehow I've felt in a kinder temper the last week than
I have for years.   So I think, Mr. Phenyl, to some
natures even bankruptcy may be a blessing.

DICK.

Well, they both begin with a B.

MRS. GILFILLIAN.

As for you, my poor brother likes you — says you
read the paper to him so intelligently.   [*Holding
out her hand to him.*]   And *I* like you.   There, sir!

DICK.

[*Taking her hand gratefully.*]   My dear aunt! I
beg your pardon — my dear Mrs. Gilfillian.

MINNIE *enters carrying two dusters.*

MRS. GILFILLIAN.

So we'll forget a week ago. Mr. Phenyl, for good.
And if at any time you feel you want — *a cup of
cocoa,* I know an old nurse who'll make it for you.
[*Taking a duster from* MINNIE.]   Come, child, let's
get rid of some of Mr. Phenyl's dust.

DICK.

[*To himself.*]   Aunt!   Who'd have thought it?
Aunt!   [*There is a rat-tat-tat at the outer door.*

MRS. GILFILLIAN.

[*In a whisper.*] We're not visible, Mr. Phenyl, to anybody.

DICK.

[*Going.*] No, certainly not.

MINNIE.

[*In a whisper.*] We're out, Mr. Phenyl — shopping.

DICK.

[*Drawing the curtain over the opening.*] I should rather think you were.   .

MINNIE.

[*To* DICK.] Hush !

> [DICK *disappears behind the curtain and opens the door, while* MRS. GILFILLIAN *and* MINNIE *stand listening.*

DICK.

[*At the door.*] How d'ye do ? How d'ye do ?

MRS. GILFILLIAN.

[*To* MINNIE, *in a whisper.*] Who is it ?

DICK.

[*Out of sight.*] No — went out shopping about ten minutes ago.

MINNIE.

[*To* MRS. GILFILLIAN.] I don't know.

DICK.

You'll find them both in the Lowther Arcade.
Oh!

[*The curtain is pushed aside and* HORACE
BREAM *enters.*

HORACE.

[*As he enters.*]   Smoke a cigar with you, Mr.
Phenyl, till they return.

MINNIE *and* MRS. GILFILLIAN.

Oh!   [MINNIE *throws away her duster.*

HORACE.

[*Seizing their hands.*]   My dear Mrs. Gilfillian!
My dear Miss Gilfillian!

[DICK *returns much discomposed, gesticu-
lating to* MRS. GILFILLIAN *and* MINNIE.

DICK.

[*Helplessly.*]   Would come in!

HORACE.

I am perfectly delighted to find that my friend
Phenyl was mistaken.   I'm much earlier to-day
than usual.

[MINNIE *embarrassed, shakes her head at*
HORACE.

MRS. GILFILLIAN.

Earlier than usual!

HORACE.

[*Not seeing* MINNIE'S *signs.*] Yes. I invariably call to inquire after Mr. Wedderburn during the afternoon.

MINNIE.

[*Turning away.*] Oh !

HORACE.

I shall be here again *this* afternoon.

MRS. GILFILLIAN.

I haven't heard of your calling at all !

MINNIE.

[*Confused.*] Oh, yes, mamma, Mr. Bream has made the — usual — inquiries during the week, generally while you have been resting. His cards are somewhere.

HORACE.

Oh, yes ; my cards are somewhere.

DR. DELANEY *enters.*

MRS. GILFILLIAN.

[*Angrily to herself, at* HORACE.] Oh, this man !
[*She goes to* DELANEY *and they talk together.*

MINNIE.

[*Eyeing* HORACE.] Oh! now he knows that mamma didn't know. [*To* HORACE *with dignity.*] I hope, Mr. Bream, that you will forgive Mr.

Phenyl's lack of candour in telling you that mamma and I were out shopping.

DICK.

[*To himself.*] Oh!

MINNIE.

Perhaps it would have been better if he had explained that we don't receive visitors at this time of trouble and anxiety.

DICK.

[*Aghast.*] I — why, you — I mean — There now.

HORACE.

[*Surprised, to* MINNIE.] Why, Minnie — [*She draws herself up and looks frowningly.*] Miss Gilfillian, I never suspected that the happy hour we have passed together every afternoon this week, has been on my part an intrusion and on yours a —

MINNIE.

Oh — I — I've made every excuse for you — knowing that you're an American. In trying to avoid formality, perhaps I've been a little — a little — a little —

HORACE.

[*Reproachfully.*] Well, a little —

[DR. DELANEY *comes over to* MINNIE.

DR. DELANEY.

[*Quietly to* MINNIE.] I've a word or two to say to Mr. Phenyl. I don't want your dear mother to hear.

[MINNIE *nods to* DR. DELANEY, *and goes to where* MRS. GILFILLIAN *is sitting.*

HORACE.

[*Following, taps* DICK *on the shoulder.*] Mr. Phenyl.

DICK.

[*Looking up.*] Eh ?

DR. DELANEY.

[*Bending over him.*] I fancy there's something worrying Mr. Wedderburn.

DICK.

Well, I should *think* so !

DR. DELANEY.

What is it ?

DICK.

Sixpence in the pound.

DR. DELANEY.

Ah, I mean something not connected with dividends at all. [*Drawing* DICK *a little nearer.*] Mr. Phenyl, I hear that Wedderburn has been rambling a little about the woman who used to live downstairs — talking about her in his sleep.

DICK.

Ah, I dare say. His boy is in love with her daughter, and that troubles him.

DR. DELANEY.

So Mrs. Gilfillian explains. But, Mr. Phenyl, doesn't it strike you as rather odd that Mr. Wedder-

burn should dream less of his bankruptcy than of
the woman whom I hear he happened to meet in
this room a week ago, and who disappeared immediately afterwards ?

DICK.

[*Startled.*]   Eh ?   Why, what — ?

DR. DELANEY.

Be quiet !

MRS. GILFILLIAN.

[*Rising.*]   Minnie, I mustn't waste my time any
longer.

DR. DELANEY.

[*Turning to the others.*]   One moment, one moment !   I've got another patient here.   Mr. Phenyl
has as much right to be ill as any of ye.

DICK.

[*To himself.*]   What's he driving at.

[MRS. GILFILLIAN, MINNIE, *and* HORACE
continue talking.

DR. DELANEY.

Now, mee dear Mr. Phenyl, you have been
acquainted with this Mrs. Rolt for many years.
Do you know her history, sir ?

DICK.

[*Agitatedly.*]   No — yes — a small portion of it.

DR. DELANEY.

Thank ye.   The small portion of a woman's history which she confides to another is generally the

Index. Now may I ask if the Index in your pos-
session goes down to the letter " W " ?

DICK.

[*Sinking into the armchair with his hand to his
forehead.*] Wedderburn! Good gracious! The
possibility never struck me! Oh!

DR. DELANEY.

But you perceive the possibility ?

DICK.

Don't pump me, Dr. Delaney, please! Confound
it, you wouldn't ask me to betray a woman's confidence, by even a hint!

DR. DELANEY.

Not for the worrld! [*Taking* DICK's *hand.*]
Besides, afther all, perhaps this is no business of
moine. Good-morning, Mr. Phenyl. [*To himself,
as he takes up his hat.*] Now, if my theory is cor-
rect I wonder if I could contrive to do a little good
to a miserable man and an unhappy woman by a
bold stroke? I'm inclined for the experiment.
Mrs. Gilfillian —

MRS. GILFILLIAN.

Yes, doctor ?

DR. DELANEY.

[*Taking her hand.*] I've been thinking I shall
have you and your pretty daughter on my hands if
I don't take better care of ye.

MRS. GILFILLIAN.

There, there — Minnie shall go into the Park
every afternoon.

DR. DELANEY.

Yes, and Minnie's mamma too. And so I've
arranged to send ye one of the dear good ladies
from my beautiful new Home.

MRS. GILFILLIAN.

Now, Doctor Delaney, I've told you —

DR. DELANEY.

[*Persuasively.*] Ah, now, just to enable you to
get the amount of fresh air which every woman in
her prime requires.

MRS. GILFILLIAN.

Well, do as you like, doctor.

DR. DELANEY.

[*Shaking hands.*] I'll do that. Good-morning.

MRS. GILFILLIAN, MINNIE, *and* HORACE.
Good-morning.

MRS. GILFILLIAN.

[*Going to* DICK.] But your nurse won't get a
very cordial reception here, I'm afraid.

DR. DELANEY.

[*To himself.*] Now that's just the point I'm a
little curious about.   [*He bustles out.*

MRS. GILFILLIAN.

I'll go to a Registry Office at once and hire a handy girl, if there's one in London. I won't have that degraded woman McOstrich in these rooms again. [*Turning sharply, she sees* MINNIE *and* HORACE *close together.*] Minnie!

> [HORACE *leaves* MINNIE *quickly, and thrusts himself half out of the window.*

MINNIE.

Mamma!

MRS. GILFILLIAN.

[*Severely.*] When Mr. Bream has terminated his visit, perhaps in this hour of emergency you will remember there is such a place as the pantry.

> [MRS. GILFILLIAN *goes into* DICK'S *room, which she is now occupying.* MINNIE *looks towards* HORACE, *whose body is half out of the window, then at* DICK, *then at her hands.*

MINNIE.

[*Sighing.*] Washing up is awfully trying for one's hands.

DICK.

I'll help — shall I?

MINNIE.

What a good-natured man you are, Mr. Phenyl! I'm so sorry I scolded you.

DICK.

Delighted.

MINNIE.

But it was quite necessary to read Mr. Bream a lesson.

DICK.

Oh, quite.

MINNIE.

But I couldn't think of allowing you to assist to wash up. I've got to be domesticated now, and I'd better begin at the degrading part.

DICK.

Well, look here — let's halve it. One of us will wash, the other will wipe.

MINNIE.

[*Glancing towards* HORACE, *abstractedly.*] It's very thoughtful of you.

DICK.

Not at all — I take it for exercise. But mind, I'm only an amateur.

MINNIE.

Not letting anything drop is the great secret. Which will you do, wash or wipe?

DICK.

I'll do the wettest — that is, the wetter of the two.

MINNIE.

You are good-natured — but both are equally unpleasant.

DICK.

Let's flutter for who does which.

MINNIE.

Flutter!

DICK.

Toss up a coin.

MINNIE.

[*Glancing towards* HORACE — *with dignity.*] Oh no, thank you, I couldn't do that. [*Seeing* HORACE *is still leaning out of the window.*] Be quick, I don't mind.

DICK.

[*Producing a penny.*] Now, then. Britannia washes, and the Queen wipes. [*Throwing up a coin, and catching it smartly — to himself.*] I'm really very much better. [*To* MINNIE.] Miss Gil-fillian — sudden death — you cry.

MINNIE.

What?

DICK.

[*Solemnly.*] Sudden death — you cry.

MINNIE.

Oh, how unkind of you to suggest such things when Uncle Geoffrey is so unwell.

DICK.

You misunderstand me! I mean, you guess — head or tail.

MINNIE.

[*With dignity.*] Oh, head please.

DICK.

[*Referring to his coin.*] Woman — you wash.

MINNIE.

[*Disappointed.*]   The other is a little drier.

DICK.

Very well, just as you like.

MINNIE.

You are a good-natured man.   [*Looking towards*
HORACE.]   Mr. Bream is oblivious of everybody's
existence.

DICK.

[*Knowingly.*]   He doesn't know that aunt—that
Mrs. Gilfillian — has gone.

MINNIE.

Mr. Phenyl!

DICK.

I didn't tell tales about you, did I?

MINNIE.

Really, Mr. Phenyl, I wish you wouldn't make
such inferences.   I won't trouble you, thank you.

[*She goes out indignantly.*

DICK.

[*Calling after her, penitently.*]   I beg your pardon,
Miss Gilfillian.   [*Disconsolately.*]   I'm always put-
ting my foot in it.   [*Snatching up a ball of wool
from the work-basket on the table, and hurling it at*
HORACE's *back.*]   It's his fault!   [*Following* MIN-
NIE.]   Miss Gilfillian.

[*DICK goes out, HORACE leaves the window
and picks up the ball of wool.*

HORACE.

Hallo! Why, *she* must have thrown this! Ah, how playful she is at times. I bear no ill-will towards Mrs. Gilfillian, but what a gay, high-spirited girl Minnie would be if she were a thoroughly qualified orphan. [*Looking round.*] I guess she's hiding around here somewhere.

> [MINNIE *appears in the passage opening, wiping a cup. She peeps into the room and comes face to face with* HORACE.

HORACE.

[*Triumphantly holding up the ball of wool.*] Ha! Ha! You imagined I didn't see you throw this, but I did.

MINNIE.

[*Coldly.*] I! Really, Mr. Bream! Excuse me, I'm occupied in the pantry.

HORACE.

May I join you in the pantry?

MINNIE.

Oh, no, certainly not; but if you'll wait here, mamma won't be long.

> [*She retires, drawing the curtain over the opening in* HORACE'S *face.*

HORACE.

[*Angrily.*] Mamma! Mamma! I am becoming desperate. I can't sleep—I can't eat—I can't live on anything but hope, and this girl is just starving me.

[*Sitting disconsolately, and looking up as* MINNIE *draws aside the curtain and enters.*

MINNIE.

Ah! [*Demurely.*] Excuse me, I've come to fetch something.

[*He rises. She goes right round the room to the table.*

HORACE.

Minnie!

MINNIE.

Mr. Bream!

[*She takes up the tray with the breakfast things — and he intercepts her.*

HORACE.

I think you are the cruellest girl in this — old country.

MINNIE.

When one meets reverses and becomes poor, one must expect to lose the good opinion of — friends.

HORACE.

[*Taking the other side of the tray and holding it with his hands over hers.*] I don't call myself a friend, Minnie.

MINNIE.

[*Sarcastically.*] Indeed? Of course one doesn't know who *are* one's friends. Oh, you are hurting my hands, Mr. Bream.

HORACE.

[*Earnestly.*] You have never permitted me to be a friend. But you know perfectly well I am a —

MINNIE.

An acquaintance.

HORACE.

No — a lover.

MINNIE.

Mr. Bream — sir !

HORACE.

[*Emphatically.*] I repeat, a lover — a lover — a lover. There, I've said it.

MINNIE.

Having said it, will you allow me to carry out the tray ?

HORACE.

Permit me ? [*He takes the tray and places it on the table. She passes him, and is going out when he turns quickly, and taking her hand draws her back into the room.*] That's not fair. You must say Yes to-day, or — I —

MINNIE.

Or you start for New York next Saturday — I know. You were going to start for New York next Saturday when we first met you, months ago, if you remember.

HORACE.

Remember! My heart keeps a diary in red ink. Why don't you like me, Minnie ?

MINNIE.

How unjust! I like you as much as I can ever like — any foreigner.

HORACE.

Foreigner !

MINNIE.

I am essentially English, you know.

HORACE.

Oh, yes. The Wedderburns were originally Scotch, I believe.

MINNIE.

Yes, I know, but —

HORACE.

And your father was an Irishman.

MINNIE.

I know — certainly — but —

HORACE.

But you're essentially English. Ah, don't make this an international question. If you marry me, I'll wear Scotch tweed, and you'll never find out the difference between —

MINNIE.

Oh, thank you. I'm deeply sensible of the honour you pay me, but I really could not marry an American.

HORACE.

Why, you don't mind flirting with one.

MINNIE.

[*Indignantly.*]   Oh !

HORACE.

You know you're a very different girl on the stairs while your mother is asleep on this sofa.

MINNIE.

And this is my reward for not disturbing mamma! Only an American would throw stairs in a girl's face.

HORACE.

Miss Gilfillian, you are like the typical English gentleman who says, "Give me a home-made watch"! Nobody does give it to him, but he pays sixty guineas for one, has his crest carved on it, and is borne down on one side with the weight of it for years. When it is not being cleaned, it enables him to lose his train. At last it is stolen from him in the crowd — so he swears a little, buys a cheap American timepiece, and lives happily. Miss Gilfillian, perhaps some day when you have won and worn your home-made husband you'll give a thought to the cheap but reliable American who has now the honour to wish you good-bye.

MINNIE.

I — I shall not say good-bye, or anything, after such — unkindness. To — to — to be called a flirt! A flirt! Oh, dear, it's so hard!

> [*She takes up the tray from the table and backs towards* HORACE, *who suddenly puts his arm round her waist.*

HORACE.

Ah, forgive me!

MINNIE.

Forgive you! After such a cruel charge! Remove your arm, Mr. Bream!

HORACE.

[*Clasping her to him.*]   I can't, Minnie, I can't.

MINNIE.

And you know *I* can't drop the tray.   [*Struggling slightly.*]   Oh, how un-English!   [*Calling.*] Mr. Phenyl!

DICK.

[*Outside.*]   Yes!

> [DICK *enters wiping a plate, and* HORACE *retreats hastily.*

MINNIE.

Take this, dear Mr. Phenyl.

DICK.

[*Taking the tray.*]   With pleasure.

> [MINNIE *looks indignantly at* HORACE. MRS. GILFILLIAN *enters, dressed for going out.*

MRS. GILFILLIAN.

[*Looking from one to the other.*]   Minnie!

MINNIE.

[*Embarrassed.*]   I — I'm teaching Mr. Phenyl how to wash up, mamma.

DICK.

[*To himself.*]   Oh, I like that!

> [DICK *carries out the tray.*

MRS. GILFILLIAN.

[*To herself.*] That young man still here. [*To
HORACE.*] Mr. Bream, I shall be much obliged if
you'll give me your arm across the Strand.

HORACE.

Certainly! It will be the last opportunity I shall
have of rendering you even so slight a service.

[MINNIE *turns, listening.*

MRS. GILFILLIAN.

Indeed!

HORACE.

1 start for N'York — [*emphatically*] — on Wednesday.   [MINNIE *gives a stifled exclamation.*

MRS. GILFILLIAN.

We're very sorry — though, perhaps, you have
been wasting your time rather sadly.

HORACE.

That notion has just struck me. Please say fare-
well for me to everybody. [MINNIE *looks at him
wistfully.*] And tell Mr. Wedderburn that I have
called every day this past week [*looking at* MIN-
NIE] solely to enquire after him.

[MINNIE *retreats to the window-seat.*

MRS. GILFILLIAN.

[*Dubiously.*] Um! I'm quite ready, Mr. Bream.
[*She goes out.*

HORACE.

[*Bowing profoundly to* MINNIE.]   Good-bye, Miss Gilfillian.

> [*She rises with downcast eyes, and makes
> him a stately courtesy.*

MINNIE.

[*In a low voice.*]   Good-bye, Mr. Bream.

> [*She resumes her seat, looking out of the
> window. He goes to the door.*

HORACE.

[*To* DICK, *shaking hands.*]   Good-bye, Mr. Phenyl: sha'n't see you again on this side, sir.

> [*He follows* MRS. GILFILLIAN; DICK *closes
> the door after them.*

MINNIE.

[*Tearfully.*]   Oh, I didn't mean it! I didn't mean it! Oh, come back, Horace! Horace!

> [*She sits at the writing-table, and writes
> rapidly. DICK comes into the room,
> polishing a teaspoon.*

DICK.

[*Eyeing* MINNIE.]   Nice girl — but I am both washing *and* wiping.

MINNIE.

[*Writing.*]   "Never — start — for New York — without me — Horace."   [*Rising with the note in her hand.*] Give me something heavy, to weight this! [*Snatching the spoon from* DICK.] That'll do.

DICK.

Eh ?

[*She screws up the spoon in the paper and runs up to the window.*]

MINNIE.

[*Looking out of the window.*] Ah! [*Calling softly.*] Horace! Horace!

[*She throws out the spoon and paper.*

DICK.

[*To himself.*] That spoon belonged to my poor mother.

MINNIE.

[*Withdrawing from the window hastily.*] Oh! Mamma's got it.

DICK.

Glad to hear it.

MINNIE.

Oh, Mr. Phenyl, run after Mr. Bream!

DICK.

[*Catching up his hat.*] Certainly. [*Giving her the cloth he carries.*] You go on with the wiping. What shall I say ?

MINNIE.

Say I want him to inquire after Uncle Geoffrey as usual.

DICK.

[*Opening the door.*] I know — half-past three on the landing.

MINNIE.

No, no! Mr. Phenyl! How dare you! [DICK *returns, leaving the door open.*] You needn't go, thank you. [*Returning to the window-seat.*] I won't humble myself! I won't!

> [LAVENDER *appears outside the door. She peeps in, then comes into the room, and, seeing* DICK, *utters a cry and advances to him.*

LAVENDER.

Mr. Phenyl!

DICK.

[*Embracing her.*] Lavvy! [*Excitedly.*] Why, Lavvy, where have you come from? where are you going to? what are you doing? where's your mother? Why don't you answer me, Lavvy? Here — what — oh!

MINNIE.

[*Coming from the window.*] Lavender!

LAVENDER.

[*Going to her.*] Oh, Miss Gilfillian! Miss Gilfillian!

MINNIE.

[*Taking* LAVENDER *in her arms — to* DICK.] Shut the door! [DICK *goes to the door and closes it.* MINNIE *places* LAVENDER *in the armchair, and removes her hat.*] Oh, poor Clement ! How happy he will be ! How happy he will be !

DICK.

[*Returning breathlessly.*] I was about to put a question to you, Lavvy. Where have you come from ? where are you —

MINNIE.

Oh, hush, Mr. Phenyl ! Lavender will tell *me.* [*Tenderly.*] Where have you come from, dear ?

DICK.

My question !

LAVENDER.

[*Faintly.*] I've come from Miss Morrison's School at Highgate, where mother took me when we left here. I — I've run away, Miss Gilfilliau.

DICK.

Run away !

MINNIE.

Hush, Mr. Phenyl !

DICK.

Yes, but run away !

MINNIE.

Be quiet !

DICK.

Run away.

MINNIE.

Hush!

DICK.

Well, but — run away. That's pretty serious.

LAVENDER.

I've seen a newspaper with something in it
about a great misfortune happening to — Mr.
Wedderburn's bank, and how his partners have
cheated and ruined him. And I know that, if Mr.
Wedderburn is poor, Mr. Hale is poor; and I can't
rest till I've found out if it's true. Is Mr. Hale
poor, Miss Gilfillian?

MINNIE.

Yes, we're all poor now, Lavvy.

LAVENDER.

Oh, Clement!

MINNIE.

Even I do the work your little hands used to do.

DICK.

I wash up.

MINNIE.

Hush, Mr. Phenyl, please.

DICK.

But why didn't you drop a line to me quietly,
Lavvy? There'll be awful trouble over this.

LAVENDER.

I began a letter to Clement yesterday, and the
girl who lent me the paper and the envelope told

Miss Morrison, who scolded me dreadfully. But I got out of the house. If it had been a prison, Miss Gilfillian, I should have got out, now that Mr. Hale is in trouble.

DICK.

Here's a pretty kettle o' fish ! You know you'll have to be sent back, Lavvy.

MINNIE.

Nothing of the kind.

LAVENDER.

I'll *go* back when I've seen him for five minutes.

MINNIE.

[*Indignantly.*] Mr. Phenyl, you're positively heartless !

DICK.

[*Piteously.*] Heartless ! *I* heartless ! You don't know what I know. I mean, I'm a man ; you're only a couple of girls — a girl and a half I may say. [*With his hand to his head.*] Oh ! where's Ruth's secret going to now !

MINNIE.

I admire your spirit, Lavender, if Mr. Phenyl doesn't.

LAVENDER.

Ah, I've no spirit at all, Miss Gilfillian. [MINNIE *takes her in her arms and caresses her.*] But mother hid me away because I was too poor and humble for Mr. Hale — and so I was a week ago. But now

everything's changed, and it would be dreadful if
he said to himself: "Lavender was taken from me
because I was rich, yet she can't find her own way
back now that I'm in need."

MINNIE.

[*Enthusiastically.*] Clem shall hear that from
your lips within an hour!

DICK.

[*Sharply.*] No, he sha'n't.

MINNIE.

[*Hotly.*] He shall, Mr. Phenyl.

LAVENDER.

Why, Mr. Phenyl, you used not to be unkind to
me.

DICK.

[*Falteringly.*] No, Lavvy, but neither of us is
your mother. We must always consult our mothers.

MINNIE.

[*Glaring at* DICK.] Where *is* your mother,
Lavvy?

DICK.

[*Glaring back at* MINNIE.] Another of my
questions!

LAVENDER.

I mustn't tell anybody — I've promised.

MINNIE.

Very well. All you require in this matter is a
friend.

DICK.

[*Putting his arm round* LAVENDER.] I quite agree with you, Miss Gilfillian — a friend.

MINNIE.

[*Putting her arm round* LAVENDER.] A protector.

DICK.

Yes, somebody who wasn't born two or three weeks ago.

MINNIE.

I'm of age.

DICK.

Well, look at *me*.

MINNIE.

But you're not a woman!

DICK.

As it happens — as it happens!

[*A gong bell is heard striking twice.*

MINNIE.

[*To* DICK, *triumphantly.*] Ha! ha! Uncle Wedderburn's bell — twice! It's for you to read the newspaper.

LAVENDER.

[*Frightened.*] Is Mr. Wedderburn here?

MINNIE.

[*Gaily.*] Yes, we're all here. Run along, Mr. Phenyl.

DICK.

[*Enraged.*]   Miss Gilfillian, you will regret this interference.

MINNIE.

[*With her arm round* LAVENDER'S *waist, saucily.*] Regret is a woman's natural food, Mr. Phenyl — she thrives on it.

DICK.

Till it becomes remorse, Miss Gilfillian.

MINNIE.

Which is only a mild form of indigestion.

DICK.

[*Furiously.*]   Oh !
[*He goes into* CLEMENT'S *room.*

MINNIE.

[*Triumphantly.*]   Ha, ha !   [*Assisting* LAVENDER *to put on her hat.*]   Now for poor Clem.

LAVENDER.

Oh, yes — where is he ?

MINNIE.

Gone to the lawyer's.   We'll run out and meet him on his way home, and then we'll sit down in the gardens.

LAVENDER.

What makes you so kind ?

MINNIE.

A fellow-feeling. I'm unhappy in my love, too.

LAVENDER.

[*Putting her arms round* MINNIE's *neck.*] Oh! Tell me.

MINNIE.

He's Mr. Bream. I said "No" to him, and he believed me, in a foolish American way he has.

LAVENDER.

Oh, we ought always to speak the truth. Why, directly Clement asked me, I said "Yes."

MINNIE.

Well, Lavvy, at a big dinner the sweets are always brought round twice, and I thought — I thought — [*Whimpering.*] I'm a wretched girl.

LAVENDER.

[*Affectionately.*] Don't cry! Don't cry!

MINNIE.

I forgot that if the sweets do come round again, other ladies have been digging spoons in.

LAVENDER.

Is he far away?

MINNIE.

Yes — he's in the Strand now.

LAVENDER.

Let us go after him with Clement.

MINNIE.

But wouldn't that look as *if* — ?

LAVENDER.

Yes, it would rather look *as if* —

MINNIE.

Oh, then, I couldn't.

LAVENDER.

Yes, but if we met him we could walk past.

MINNIE.

[*Hugging* LAVENDER.] Oh, you darling! I'm so fond of you.

The door of CLEMENT'S *room opens, and* GEOFFREY WEDDERBURN *enters, followed by* DICK, *carrying some books and newspapers under his arm.* WEDDERBURN *looks much older than before, his hair being grey and his voice and manner feeble.*

MINNIE.

[*To* LAVENDER.] Uncle Geoffrey!

LAVENDER.

[*Clinging to* MINNIE.] Oh!

DICK.

[*To himself.*] Oh, dear!

[DICK *waves the girls away.* WEDDER-
BURN *walks slowly.*

WEDDERBURN.

[*Seeing* MINNIE.] Ah, Minnie, my dear.

MINNIE.

[*Going to him.*] Why, uncle!

WEDDERBURN.

[*Patting her cheek.*] Ah, I can't submit to be nursed and cosseted any longer. I — I — shall go down to Barnchester to-morrow to face the people, and — and to see about other things. [*Seeing* LAVENDER.] Who's that young lady, my dear?

MINNIE.

[*Bringing* LAVENDER *forward.*] This is — a friend of mine, uncle.

> [WEDDERBURN *holds out his hand.* LAV- ENDER *puts her hand in his, timidly.*]

WEDDERBURN.

I'm very glad to see Minnie's friend.

LAVENDER.

[*With a courtesy.*] Thank you, sir.

WEDDERBURN.

I've been rather ill, my dear, but the doctor says I may go into the gardens while the sun is out. Will you walk on one side of me, with Minnie on the other?

LAVENDER.

I — I would, sir — if my mother would let me.

WEDDERBURN.

Your mamma will let you if she's a kind mamma.
If not, I shall have to put up with Mr. Richard.

[DICK *assists* WEDDERBURN *into the armchair.*

WEDDERBURN.

[*Gratefully, to* DICK.] And Mr. Richard's a
dreadful fellow — such a bear. Aren't you, Richard — eh ?

MINNIE.

[*In a whisper to* LAVENDER, *pointing to the door
of* DICK'S *room.*] That's my room, now. Come
with me.   [*The two girls go out quietly.*

DICK.

[*To himself looking after* MINNIE *and* LAVEN-
DER.] Girls will do anything. I begin to have a
better opinion of myself, now that I've mixed more
with girls.

WEDDERBURN.

Now, then, Mr. Richard.

DICK.

[*Taking up a newspaper.*] What'll you have, sir?

WEDDERBURN.

Anything referring to the failure of Wedderburn's bank ?

DICK.

[*Opening the paper uncomfortably. To himself.*] Ahem! This daily invention of favourable comments on Wedderburn's neglect of his business rather taxes my imagination. Ready, sir?

WEDDERBURN.

Yes, yes, Mr. Richard.

DICK.

H'm! [*To himself.*] Hallo! Here *is* a short leader. [*Reading.*] "It will not be difficult to find an excuse for Mr. Wedderburn's ignorance of the affairs of the bank."

WEDDERBURN.

[*Eagerly.*] Ah! That's good — that's just.

DICK.

[*To himself.*] It *will* be difficult, they say here. Wonderful what a word does.

[*There is a rat-tat-tat at the outer door.*

DICK.

[*Laying down the paper.*] Excuse me.

WEDDERBURN.

[*To himself.*] It will not be difficult to find an excuse for Mr. Wedderburn — an excuse for Mr. Wedderburn.

[DICK *opens the door.* DR. DELANEY *and* RUTH, *dressed as a nurse, but veiled, are outside.*

DR. DELANEY.

Thank ye, Mr. Phenyl. Thank ye. [*Cheerily, pointing to* WEDDERBURN.] Come, now, look at that! That's the sort of constitution that's the ruin of my profession.

[DICK *closes the door.* RUTH *touches his arm.*

RUTH.

[*In a whisper.*] Mr. Phenyl!

DICK.

Ruth!

DR. DELANEY.

Wedderburn, I've brought ye a lady from my new Home, just as a companion for your sister and Minnie. I've told ye about my beautiful Home.

WEDDERBURN.

Thank you, Delaney, but I'm quite strong now.

DR. DELANEY.

I know that — but it's you strong chaps that require looking after. Think of the ladies — they're getting as white as the ceiling; and poor Mr. Phenyl, who's hoarse with reading aloud to you. Mr. Phenyl. [*Beckoning to* DICK.

WEDDERBURN.

[*Feebly to* RUTH.] I hope I wasn't discourteous, ma'am. Every one is very good to me — very good to me.

RUTH.

[*In a low voice.*] Mr. Wedderburn.

[WEDDERBURN *starts and looks up.*

WEDDERBURN.

[*In a whisper.*] Who is it ?

RUTH.

Ruth.

WEDDERBURN.

Ruth — Ruth !

RUTH.

I am the nurse that Doctor Delaney speaks of. Do you wish me to remain, Mr. Wedderburn ?

WEDDERBURN.

[*With an effort, in a low voice.*] Yes, Ruth.

[*He sinks back into his chair, staring forward. She removes her bonnet and cloak.*

DR. DELANEY.

[*Softly to* DICK.] That's all right. [*Aloud.*] I'll be with ye again in ten minutes, Wedderburn. [*Nudging* DICK.] A delicate, but successful experiment. Come, I'll tell ye how I put the pieces of the puzzle together.

[DICK *and* DELANEY *go into the other room.*

RUTH.

If Mr. Phenyl was reading to you shall I take his place ?

WEDDERBURN.

[*Passing his hand across his brow.*] You are merciful to me, Ruth. You come to me when I am ill, broken, in misfortune.

RUTH.

It is my calling now to soften pain, to try to banish suffering.

WEDDERBURN.

But I — I ruined your life for you. Do you forget that ?

RUTH.

No — I remember it. A week ago I had every reason to fly from this house, where I had lived undisturbed and peacefully for so many years; but when the good doctor told me you were lying here, stricken down, I remembered — I remembered.

[*Covering her face with her hands.*

WEDDERBURN.

Ruth, my girl.

RUTH.

[*Recovering herself, and laying her hand upon his arm.*] Ah, I am forgetting why I am here. The doctor will scold me.

WEDDERBURN.

For what ? For helping to ease my heart ? Ruth, I have suffered. I have stared the world in the face as if I were an honest man, and bragged of my shrewdness and hard common-sense. I have only been playing a loud tune to drown my conscience. I — I have suffered.

RUTH.

Hush, Mr. Wedderburn, hush! Not now!

WEDDERBURN.

Ruth, I have never forgotten the woman I betrayed and broke my promise to, eighteen years since. I have never forgotten the time when you asked me if I was ashamed of the poor girl who hung upon my arm in the lanes about Barnchester, and the answer I gave you. Your look of shame and reproach as you left me has been always with me, and it was the ghost of that look which struck me down here, a week ago.

[*Burying his face in his handkerchief.*

RUTH.

You've been too hard upon yourself, Mr. Wedderburn. You were right — I was not a fit wife for you. And now we are growing old! Forget it and suffer no more.

[*She breaks down and leans her head upon the back of the chair, weeping.*]

WEDDERBURN.

But why talk of my sufferings, Ruth? What have yours been?

RUTH.

Less than I deserved — because you know, sir, Heaven had mercy upon me, and consoled me.

WEDDERBURN.

Ah! I remember. They call you Mrs. Rolt here —you were Ruth Rawdon at Barnchester. You

are a widow, with a daughter whom Clement has
become attached to.   I remember.

[*She goes back a step or two, staring at him.*

RUTH.

[*Under her breath.*]   Mr. Wedderburn — I am
not a widow — I have never married.

WEDDERBURN.

Never — married.

RUTH.

[*With a low cry.*]   Oh, Mr. Wedderburn!   I call
myself a widow to keep my child ignorant of my
disgrace.   It would kill me for her to know.   [*In a
whisper.*]   But — Lavender is more than seventeen
years old.

WEDDERBURN.

[*Repeating the words to himself.*]   More than
seventeen years old.   [*Looking at her for a moment,
then stretching out his arms appealingly.*]   Ruth —
Ruth!   Tell me!   [*She slowly sinks on her knees
beside him.*]

RUTH.

Geoffrey, I thought you guessed I had been
faithful to my first love.   I took my secret with
me from Barnchester, because I was too proud to
beg for compassion; but when you found mother
and child here, you might have guessed the truth.
[*Turning away, weeping.*]   Ah, how lightly you've
always thought of me!

WEDDERBURN.

[*Taking her hand.*] Ruth, I am utterly bank-
rupt. I have lost strength, fortune, comfort — all
that makes age endurable. But what I've lost now
is little compared to what I flung away eighteen
years ago — the love of a faithful woman.

LAVENDER *enters with* MINNIE, *both dressed
for going out.*

RUTH.

Lavender!

LAVENDER.

[*Going to* RUTH.] Mother, dear mother, don't be
angry with me! Mother!

WEDDERBURN.

[*In a whisper to himself, sinking into the armchair.*] My child!

CLEMENT *enters hurriedly.*

MINNIE.

[*Running up to him.*] Clement! Look here!

[LAVENDER *goes to* CLEMENT *and clings to
him.*

CLEMENT.

Lavender! Mrs. Rolt!

LAVENDER.

Ah, Clement!

DICK *and* DR. DELANEY *enter.*

LAVENDER.

[*Passionately.*] Mother! I read that Mr. Hale had become poor, and I came here this morning to ask if it was true. It is true! There's no reason for separating us now. Clement, no one shall take me away again if you wish me to stay. I'll be poor with you. I'll share all your struggles. I'll slave for you, I'll be a true patient companion. And if ever you're rich again, and tire of me, as they say you will, I'll remember the days when you loved me, and won't complain — I promise. Mother, you mustn't treat me as a child any longer — I'm a woman. I can't go back to Miss Morrison's! I won't! Clement, keep me with you! Keep me with you! Keep me with you!

[*There is a knock at the door.*

CLEMENT.

[*Putting his arm round her.*] For ever, Lavender, for ever. Father, you hear! Father!

[LAVENDER *sits in the window recess with* CLEMENT, *and they are joined by* DICK *and* DR. DELANEY. *There is another knock at the door,* MINNIE *opens it, and* MRS. GIL-FILLIAN *enters, followed by* HORACE.

MINNIE.

Mamma! Oh, look here!

MRS. GILFILLIAN.

Mrs. Rolt!

MINNIE.

[*Seeing* HORACE.] Oh, Horace! Horace!

[*She embraces* HORACE *impulsively.*

MRS. GILFILLIAN.

Good gracious me! Why, Mrs. Rolt, you're surely not the nurse Doctor Delaney promised us?

DR. DELANEY.

[*Going to* MRS. GILFILLIAN *and taking her hands.*] Mee dear lady, with the acuteness which is your characteristic, you've hit it. Mrs. Rolt came into my beautiful Home a week ago. She didn't wish it known, and it was no business of moine to divulge it. But when I wanted to preserve the roses in your own cheeks, ma'am, it was Mrs. Rolt who volunteered to help in a work for which all humanity should be grateful.

MRS. GILFILLIAN.

[*To* RUTH, *shaking hands with her.*] Well, I'm sure I'm much obliged to Mrs. Rolt. [*Looking round and discovering* LAVENDER.] Why, here's your daughter!

DR. DELANEY.

Oh, yes, ma'am, we allow beautiful flowers in a sick room — [*pointing to the window*] — if you keep the window open.

RUTH.

[*Falteringly.*] I — I did my best. Lavender has been away — at school.

DR. DELANEY.

But the poor little thing chirrups for her mother — hen and chick, ma'am.

MRS. GILFILLIAN.

[*Dubiously.*] Um — and she follows you here. A coincidence.

DR. DELANEY.

[*Stroking his chin.*] Coincidences occur in the best regulated families. The most delightful part of this one is that Mrs. Rolt happens to be an old acquaintance of Mr. Wedderburn's.

MRS. GILFILLIAN.

Old — old acquaintance?

WEDDERBURN.

Yes, Clara, an old acquaintance. [*He rises, supporting himself upon* RUTH's *arm.*] Clement — Lavender!

RUTH.

[*Softly to* WEDDERBURN.] My secret, my secret! You'll not —

[CLEMENT *and* LAVENDER *come to them.*

WEDDERBURN.

[*Falteringly.*] Clara, my dear boy, and you, my dear girl, it is quite true. I knew Mrs. Rolt years ago, when she was — unmarried. This lady did me the honour to believe in me, to love me, until, very wisely, she perceived that I was not worth her devotion — and we parted. But, Clement, you are wiser, better, braver than I was. Boy as you are, you have secured the prize I missed, by discovering that the only rank which elevates a woman is that which a gentle spirit bestows upon her. Lavender, my dear, come here. [*Taking her hand as she comes to him timidly.*] Lavender, you will be my boy's wife, so you must try to forgive my old unkindness to your mother, and learn to call me father.

> [*He draws her to him and kisses her. Then*
> RUTH *takes* LAVENDER *aside.*

CLEMENT.

[*To* WEDDERBURN.] Ah, dad, didn't I describe her faithfully ? Isn't she sweet and good ?

WEDDERBURN.

Yes, Clement; but, Clara, what are we to say to Minnie ?

MRS. GILFILLIAN.

[*Testily.*] There, don't talk about Minnie! I wash my hands of her and everybody else. It appears I know nothing about anyone or anything. I ought to have been buried years ago. As for my daughter, she throws a letter out of a window addressed to a gentleman — it falls into my hands, and I, having left my spectacles at home, actually ask that very gentleman to read it. Don't talk to me, anybody.

MINNIE.

Don't be sorry about me, Uncle Geoffrey. Of course, I've been very fond of Clem for many years, but — I'm engaged to Mr. Bream, now.

WEDDERBURN.

To Mr. Bream ?

MINNIE.

[*Looking towards* HORACE.] Horace! Advance!

WEDDERBURN.

And how long has this been going on?

HORACE.

Well, it has been going backwards and forwards and all round for some months, but it has only been going *on* for about —

MRS. GILFILLIAN.

For about ten minutes!

HORACE.

[*To* DICK.] Mr. Phenyl. [*Returning the tea-spoon.*] I am eternally obliged to you — your property, I believe.

DICK.

Oh, thank you. [*Looking at the spoon.*] Bad omen! Dented!

> [*There's a rat-tat at the door.* CLEMENT *opens the door and admits* MR. MAW.

CLEMENT.

Dad, here's Mr. Maw with the news!

MAW.

[*Breathlessly going to* WEDDERBURN *and shaking hands with him.*] Mr. Wedderburn, I am pleased, I am delighted to acquaint you with the result of the private meeting of the creditors of the Barnchester Bank. [*To* DICK, *who is walking away.*] Ah, don't go, Mr. Phenyl, please.

DICK.

[*Coming to* MAW, *uneasily.*] Awfully busy — back in five minutes.

MAW.

[*Holding his arm.*] No, no. The principal creditors, animated by the example of one of their number, have resolved to put Wedderburn's Bank upon its legs again — with every prospect of restoring confidence, sir, and discharging its old responsibilities.

WEDDERBURN.

Mr. Maw!

MAW.

And who do you think has turned the tide of Barnchester opinion in your favour, sir? [*Pointing to* DICK.] Mr. Phenyl, who has formally acquitted the Bank of the liability of the amount of the late Mr. Vipont's fortune.

WEDDERBURN.

Richard! [DICK *comes to* WEDDERBURN, *who takes his hand, and sinks back into the armchair.* RUTH *comes quickly to* WEDDERBURN.]

MRS. GILFILLIAN.

[*Throwing her arms round* DICK's *neck.*] Oh, Mr. Phenyl!

DICK.

[*Uncomfortably.*] Thank you — thank you.

MRS. GILFILLIAN.

Oh, what a lot of good there is in you! [*Still clinging to* DICK.] Be quiet! Let me have my cry out.

DICK.

[*Quietly to* CLEMENT.] Clement, my boy — aunt!

CLEMENT.

[*To* LAVENDER.] What did I always say Dick was!

HORACE.

Mr. Phenyl, you are worthy of our side.

MINNIE.

[*Impulsively kissing* DICK.] Dear Mr. Phenyl.

DICK.

Thank you — thank you. [*Leading her across to* HORACE.] I beg your pardon.

WEDDERBURN.

Mr. Phenyl — Richard — you will not, I hope, refuse to make your home with us at Barnchester. We live to repay you for your sacrifice, and we shall never cease to point to you as our best friend.

DICK.

Thank you, Mr. Wedderburn, but I've no fancy for the searching light of the country. Notwithstanding some slight moral repairs, the seams of my coat are prematurely white, my character radically out at elbow. If you choose to continue my acquaintance, you will find me here; and if you'll be seen with me abroad, why, we'll walk down Fleet Street.

HORACE.

I share your devotion to this old city, Mr. Phenyl. London has given me the most fascinating companion.

DR. DELANEY.

London, sir! Why, London contains the largest number of patients of any civilised city in the world.

MRS. GILFILLIAN.

And the best-hearted doctors in the world.

MINNIE.

It is always very full of Americans. [*Putting her hand in* HORACE'S.] And some people like Americans.

WEDDERBURN.

Yes, yes, we'll speak well of London. For in this overgrown tangle some flowers find strength to raise their heads — the flowers of hope and atonement. [*Taking* RUTH'S *hand and holding it. To* LAVENDER.] What do you think, my child?

LAVENDER.

I think, sir — [*going towards* CLEMENT] — whatever Clement thinks, always.

CLEMENT.

And I agree with you, father — London is a most

beautiful garden. [*Taking* DICK's *hand.*] Hasn't it grown Dick here? [*Drawing* LAVENDER *to him.*] And ah, dad! you can even pluck sweet Lavender in the Temple.

THE END.